"And what do you want?" Adam asked

His question seemed casual as he drove out of the car park into the flow of Paris traffic, but Kit wasn't deceived.

"Out-of-date, old-fashioned love," she answered defiantly. "The sort in books. It exists. It isn't based on sex alone, it's based on caring and sharing. It lasts to eternity because it's solid and real."

"I'll never get married," Adam said calmly. "I don't believe in it."

"You don't believe in anything much at all, do you? Love or friendship."

Adam was suddenly angry. "I do believe in love. It's marriage I don't believe in."

"Love? You call your sexual acrobatics love?" Kit was angry, too. "I don't want to hear another word about it!"

"Right." Adam's voice was grim. "From now on we're just working colleagues. . . ."

D0830514

Charlotte Lamb began to write "because it was one job I could do without having to leave the children." Now writing is her profession. She has had more than forty Harlequin novels published since 1978. "I love to write," she explains, "and it comes very easily to me." Once she begins a story, the plot, the actions and personalities of her characters develop almost spontaneously. She and her family live in a beautiful old home on the Isle of Man. Charlotte spends eight hours a day working at her typewriter—and she enjoys every minute of it.

Books by Charlotte Lamb

A VIOLATION
SECRETS

HARLEQUIN ROMANCE
2181—MASTER OF COMUS
2206—DESERT BARBARIAN
2696—KINGFISHER MORNING

HARLEQUIN PRESENTS
668—DARKNESS OF THE HEART
700—INFATUATION
731—SCANDALOUS
747—A NAKED FLAME
762—FOR ADULTS ONLY
772—LOVE GAMES
827—MAN HUNT
842—WHO'S BEEN SLEEPING IN MY BED
851—SLEEPING DESIRE
874—THE BRIDE SAID NO

These books may be available at your local bookseller.

Don't miss any of our special offers. Write to us at the following address for information on our newest releases.

Harlequin Reader Service
901 Fuhrmann Blvd., P.O. Box 1397, Buffalo, NY 14240
Canadian address: P.O. Box 603,
Fort Erie, Ont. L2A 9Z9

The Heron Quest

Charlotte Lamb

Harlequin Books

TORONTO • NEW YORK • LONDON
AMSTERDAM • PARIS • SYDNEY • HAMBURG
STOCKHOLM • ATHENS • TOKYO • MILAN

Original hardcover edition published in 1977
by Mills & Boon Limited

ISBN 0-373-02804-0

Harlequin Romance first edition December 1986

Printed in U.S.A.

CHAPTER ONE

THE small white sports car raced along the drive, taking the bend under the lime trees at about sixty miles an hour with a screech of tortured tyres. White dust blew up in a cloud, dispersed slowly and settled in a fire layer over the green leaves and sturdy boles of the lime trees. A blackbird rose, chinking angrily. A wood pigeon fluttered upwards too, his usual purring note becoming a squawk. The tranquil leisure of an English summer Sunday was ripped apart as the little car came towards the house.

On the lawn beside the building a man lay at ease in a striped deck chair. He raised his head at the race of the approaching engine, languidly took off the metallic sunglasses he wore and glanced across the smooth expanse of groomed green turf just as the white car drew up beside the front door.

Its driver got out, slammed the car door, mounted the three stone steps to the front door, then turned and looked back over the garden. Her eyes drifted over the man in the deck chair. They made no acknowledging gesture to each other, but the girl's fine brows drew together and her face hardened. The man lay back, his lean face once more expressionless, the sunglasses an impenetrable barrier she could not probe.

A short, dark-haired woman in a blue overall opened the front door, smiling at the newcomer in a familiar, friendly fashion. "Oh, it's you, Katherine! How are you this morning? Beautiful day, isn't it? Real June weather. J.K. is in the breakfast room."

Kit lifted an eyebrow enquiringly. "At this hour? What's up? He usually has breakfast at something approaching dawn. Don't tell me... an all-night confab with Mastermind? I saw him lounging out there on the lawn as I arrived, I felt like turning the hose on him. Even at a distance that sleek, supercilious manner gets my goat. He looked too damned pleased with himself behind those sunglasses he wears."

"There was a late-night conference," admitted the other woman hesitantly.

"Just J.K. and Adam Rothbury? Or did they have the whole ghastly crew down here?"

"Just the two of them."

"Good or bad news, Sammy?" Kit watched her curiously. "Don't pretend you don't know! You always know everything. Like the Roman soothsayers who used to read the future in the entrails of chickens, you have your own method of finding out what's going on..."

Sammy's round, comfortable face screwed up in distaste. "Entrails of chickens? Ugh...what a beastly idea!"

"Yes, foul," punned Kit, giggling.

Sammy threw up her hands. "What a terrible joke! Go on in and see J.K. He knows you're here. Nobody could miss the racket that car of yours makes. I wish you wouldn't drive so fast."

Kit eyed her suspiciously. "You're evading my question, aren't you? I don't like the sound of this..."

"J.K. will be waiting," Sammy urged, turning away.

"Bring me some fresh coffee, will you, Sammy, please? I'm parched." Kit grinned at her appealingly and vanished towards a small room at the end of the high-ceilinged hall.

The room was a sunny, white-walled rectangle. A small square table covered by a yellow-checked cloth occupied the space beside the window. Outside smooth lawns sloped down to a grass court for tennis, a well-kept croquet lawn and beyond both a narrow stream fringed by willows.

"Every prospect pleases," quoted the man seated at the table as he turned his head to smile.

"Hello, darling," Kit said, coming to kiss him. "I saw the vile man outside as I drove up. What are you two up to now? Why the sudden summons? I meant to spend my Sunday peacefully on the river with Edward. I left him sulking like mad—he'd packed a picnic and spent hours getting his boat shipshape, and then you summoned me away and ruined everything. I might have known that foul fiend Adam Rothbury was behind it somewhere!"

"You've got it wrong," J.K. demurred. "It was entirely my idea. Indeed, Adam protested in the strongest terms at having you on the job..."

"Oh, did he?" Kit bristled at once. She perched on the chair facing her uncle. "Well, cough, angel. Let me have it. What are you planning now?"

J.K. Ashley surveyed her with affectionate amusement before he spoke. Slight, slender, with a boyish figure which was yet extremely feminine, she had a strong resemblance to his dead mother which grew stronger with each passing year. Her own father and mother having been killed in a plane crash ten years ago, Katherine had moved in with him here at Sweetdown, bringing with her all the expected clutter and crises of a teenager, destroying the ordered calm of his bachelor existence as he had feared. What he had not anticipated, as he reluctantly awaited her arrival, was the new interest she would bring him; he had gradually found Kit weaving herself inextricably into his life, and he had been astonished to find himself happy with his responsibilities.

Even Sammy, the widow who had run his house for five years before Katherine's arrival, had been deeply affected. J.K. had always known her formally as Mrs Samson until Kit, before twenty-four hours was up, had begun to call her "Sammy". Horrified, J.K. had expected Mrs Samson to resign. She had always kept her distance, remained politely formal. But she had accepted the nickname cheerfully enough, and if J.K. was unaware of the reason for it, he was grateful that she should. Sammy never told him how many nights she had had to creep into Kit's room, awakened by muffled sobbing from the girl. Kit's waking liveliness disguised her grief for her parents from J.K., but not from a woman's quick eye.

It was fortunate that Kit was happily settled down at a boarding school before she was orphaned. The security and stability the school afforded helped her as much as Sammy had, and she came through that period with less stress than might have been expected.

After school she had chosen to go to a good university, to read English, and she had achieved a satisfactory if not brilliant degree. Then she had chosen to enter J.K.'s television company as a P.A., or Production Assistant, a job somewhat similar to that of teaboy on a newspaper. For six months she had run errands for the producer to whom she had been assigned. She had posted his letters, taken his telephone calls, brought him tea or coffee, soothed down his wife, sent roses to his mistress, arranged trips to the Zoo for his children and rushed to Fortnum and Mason in a taxi once a month to buy Beluga caviar for his wife's dinner parties. In between these exhausting tasks she had managed to learn something about television—not much, but something.

Intensely curious by nature, tenacious in character, she had watched, listened, learnt whenever she had the opportunity.

She had learnt how to splice tape, how to operate control panels in the studios, she had picked up technical language which at first baffled and disorientated her, until now she hardly stopped to think about fish eye lenses or P as B (the shorthand expression meaning the programme as broadcast, a list of items intended for the costing department who have to pay the bills in the end).

At this stage in her development she was offered a job with a more senior producer, Tom Leet, a choleric but brilliant documentary man who had taught her with the slave-driving intensity of a man obsessed with his world. She hated and respected him at the end of the year, but she had learnt faster than J.K. had expected.

Often J.K. had seen her at a distance, her fragile body hurtling along corridors, burdened by a pile of

cans containing film, her red-gold curls bouncing
around her face, a frown of concentration making her
look like a worried child. Now and then she waved and
a brilliant smile lit her greenish eyes, and it was at
those moments that her uncle knew how much he
loved her, by the warmth that invaded his heart at that
smile.

Quick, deft, eager, she made friends despite the
undercurrent of suspicion that she had had her path
smoothed by being J.K.'s niece. She was too cheerful,
hardworking and easy to talk to for that attitude to
persist for long, except with certain disgruntled members of the staff who wanted some scapegoat on which
to pin their own failure.

From Tom Leet she had passed on to work more
independently, as a writer-producer in the documentary department, under the general aegis of Adam
Rothbury. From the first Kit had loathed her boss. He
was sarcastic, icy and reserved. She knew that he still
suspected her of being a Trojan Horse insinuated into
his department by J.K. He had unfortunately seen her
once or twice on social occasions in the first week of
their acquaintance, and had apparently formed an
impression of her as a social butterfly without brains.
Kit's cheerful exuberance sometimes gave that
impression to strangers. It had never irked her so
much before. She grew fiercely determined to make
Adam Rothbury sit up and take notice.

She burned the midnight oil night after night, in the
little flat she had moved into after leaving Sweetdown
on her twenty-first birthday. J.K. had protested at her
decision to leave, but she was determined to be inde-
pendent. "You've had me round your neck long

enough, darling. A little peace and quiet will do you good. And if you ever need me I shall be on the end of a phone, don't forget? I'll come like a shot, I promise."

Her hard work and determination had won her grudging approval from Adam Rothbury in the end, but, typically, the man remained at a distance from her, his mocking tongue a constant threat to her peace of mind. "He makes me want to hit him," she said once to Edward Montague, the sleek-suited, smiling young architect who was her most constant companion in her leisure hours. "But I refuse to be tempted! I'm sure that's what he wants! He would like me to put myself in the wrong by slamming a handbag in his face, but I won't!"

Edward had laughed, "I shouldn't, Kit. I've a shrewd suspicion Adam Rothbury is the type to hit back—good and hard."

"I'm sure he is," she had agreed wryly.

J.K. was silent so long, in the sunny breakfast room, his mind swarming with old memories and new misgivings, that Kit grew quite anxious. "Come on, Uncle. What have you and Rothbury cooked up now between you? Some devil's brew, no doubt. Anything that sarcastic beast dreams up has to be devilish..."

"Thanks for the compliment," drawled the man in question from the door.

She stiffened, but turned very slowly, defiance in every line. He was leaning against the door frame in a negligent attitude, one hand thrust into his trouser pocket. Very tall, lean, yet with a build somehow quietly suggestive of wiry strength, he had smoothly brushed dark hair and cool grey eyes, now no longer hidden by sunglasses. His long, straight nose had an arrogant cast underlined by the firmly moulded lips and strong jaw. Even at a casual glance he was not a man to quarrel with—Kit already knew from bitter experience that he was a notable adversary, hard and unyielding, quite without gallantry. He gave and asked no quarter. She both resented and reluctantly admired him.

"Eavesdroppers hear no good of themselves," she flung at him defiantly.

"You have a very penetrating voice. I couldn't fail to hear every word," he said calmly.

"Come in and sit down, Adam," J.K. grinned, visibly enjoying this cut and thrust.

Adam strolled across the room and flung himself languidly down into a small brocade armchair, his white shirt open at the neck to display his bronzed throat. Kit eyed him resentfully. He had no damned right to be so physically attractive, she thought, when he was so unbearably irritating in other ways. She was still young enough to react with angry pride to mockery, and Adam used that particular weapon frequently. It amused him to see her react like an angry cat, her spine prickling, her hair seeming to stand on end, the green eyes flashing sparks at him.

They clashed on a number of points in their daily work. Kit had a deep sense of personal integrity which made her particularly sensitive to any charge of invasion of privacy, and as any form of television documentary can have this charge laid against it, she was always coming up against a division of interest in her work. Adam was ruthlessly committed to the pursuit of the truth above all. No protest influenced him.

When Kit anxiously questioned whether they had the right to expose the private lives of their victims, Adam would shrug coolly and ask, "How else can we get at the truth?"

J.K. murmured gently, "Kit? Shall we begin?"

She flushed scarlet, aware that she had been staring at Adam without realising it. "Yes, of course," she said hurriedly.

Sammy came in with the coffee, providing Kit with a chance to jump up and help her, covering her embarrassment with action. Sammy quietly left. They all settled down with their coffee.

"Right," said J.K. "I'll sketch in the background first. Kit, you remember we were in the middle of a series of programmes about Second World War writers? Harry Somerby was making them?"

She nodded. She had met Somerby a couple of times, and did not like him. He was a small, irascible man with protuberant eyes. His manners were appalling, his programmes were frequently dull. He had a certain ability, however, to lay out facts so that they were easily assimilated, and it was that which had given him his place on the documentary team.

"Harry was killed yesterday," J.K. said flatly. "Car crash. Silly fool was doing eighty on the motorway. Luckily, no other car was involved. We shall miss him."

"Oh, dear, poor Harry," Kit said, ashamed of her previous dislike for the dead man.

Adam, watching her small, expressive face, looked suddenly amused. Every emotion was written there so clearly. He enjoyed watching her reactions. Quietly he said, "Of course, the documentaries on World War

Two writers are half finished. Someone will have to take over."

She looked eagerly at her uncle. "Oh?"

Adam grinned. "J.K. suggests you do them..."

Her eyes widened excitedly and she caught her breath. "On my own? Without you?"

"That appeals to you, does it?" Adam mocked.

"I would like the chance to prove myself," she defended.

J.K. glanced at Adam. "Naturally," he murmured. "Adam, where is the research file on Jan Watowski?"

Adam moved gracefully to a table on the other side of the room, returned with the blue cardboard file and handed it to J.K. "All we have is in there," he said.

J.K. looked at Kit. She was frowning. "You've heard of Watowski?" he asked.

"Vaguely. He was Polish, wasn't he?"

J.K. nodded. "A Polish pilot who flew with the Royal Air Force, yes. He was killed in 1942. Crashed over Kent. His poems were brought out posthumously by Saxton Landell, the critic."

"Landell's been living off them ever since," Adam said drily. "He made his name with his book on Watowski."

"But what's so special about him? I've never even read a line of Watowski. Why are we including him in our list of writers?"

"Good question," J.K. said, smiling.

"And the answer," murmured Adam, "is that from being a total unknown twenty years ago, Watowski has somehow slowly crept up the popularity charts to an astonishing height. He seems to have become a cult figure with the universities to start with—they went for his Byronic cynicism in a big way, but he's much more complex than that...underneath the mockery he pretends to feel, one gradually senses a wildly romantic spirit. He's a strange combination. In the last five years he's sold solidly. His publishers are Grant & Yates, and they've been quick to catch on to what was happening. They're bringing out a new edition of the poems for his thirty-fifth anniversary. They're throwing a grand luncheon party at the Hilton and making as big a splash as possible.''

''Do you think he's that good?'' Kit asked him.

Adam looked at her consideringly. ''I'm not sure. Sometimes he touches a nerve. At other times I suspect he's pulling some sort of fast one on the reader...but I'm not certain about him at all. I can see why young people go for him. He was only twenty when he died, after all. He was wild, reckless, rather charming, if Saxton Landell is to be believed.''

''How much of his popularity is due to what this Landell has written about him?'' Kit asked.

Adam's long mouth twitched. He glanced at J.K. ''This child can sometimes put her finger on the tender spot with unnerving accuracy,'' he drawled.

''Don't patronise me!'' Kit flared.

Adam raised one eyebrow languidly. ''My dear child...''

''I'm not a child!''

The grey eyes flicked disparagingly over her. ''No? Appearances can be deceptive, of course...''

She bit her lip, raging helplessly. She never seemed to win in these exchanges.

"I was paying you a compliment," Adam pointed out. "You shrewdly picked out the weak spot in this Watowski business. Everything we know about him comes from Landell's book. The poems certainly fit in with Landell's picture of him, but there are a few poems which are puzzling. It occurred to me, when I'd read the file Harry Somerby had got together, that Watowski would stand for a little more in-depth probing. There must be people who knew him...people who didn't talk to Landell. The boy was over here for two years before he died, and in those days a week was a lifetime. Watowski must have put in a lot of living before he died."

Kit was flushed and excited. "It sounds interesting! Is that what you want me to do? Play detective and find out all I can about Watowski?"

Adam gazed at her calmly. "You think you could handle it on your own?"

"You said Harry had already researched him? I suppose he put the team on the job?"

The research team was run by a formidable lady known as Martha to half the world. She was direct, friendly, tenacious, and never failed to bring back a story.

"Martha did her usual good job, but I want more than that, with this one," Adam said.

"Fine," Kit nodded. "When shall I start? Tomorrow?"

"We'll start on Wednesday," Adam said softly.

"We?" Kit stiffened.

"I want to be in on this one," he said. "I have a sort of personal stake. Watowski fascinates me. I have... let's say a hunch...about him."

Kit looked at her uncle uncertainly. He was listening without expression. "But I thought you were going on holiday," she protested.

"I am," Adam nodded. "A busman's holiday. This is going to take us all over England. Watowski was based in various parts of the country during his two years."

Kit felt a tingle of warning down her spine. She glanced at J.K. appealingly. "I'm sure Adam is too busy to take off like this," she said. "What about the Capitalism series?"

"In the can," Adam said sweetly. "I've wrapped it up nicely in pretty pink ribbons and it's all finished. So I'm free, and J.K. has agreed that I can please myself over this one..."

"Why did you give me the impression I was going to be doing it?" she asked sulkily.

"You're going along with Adam as his P.A.," her uncle said. "My dear girl, you aren't experienced enough to do this entirely alone! It was Adam's idea, Adam's programme. I wanted you to go along for the experience. You've never worked out in the field before, you've only worked in the studio or the office. You'll learn a lot from watching Adam at work."

"I'm sure I shall," she said icily.

Adam grinned at her tone. "I've fixed an interview with Landell for Wednesday," he told her.

"Oh? I thought you wanted to bypass him?"

"Don't be an idiot, he can give us some useful introductions," Adam said. "Harry's programme would merely have covered all the old, well-tilled ground. He relied heavily on Landell. But I want to dig up new stuff, and to do that I have to start with Landell. I do not, however, want Landell to suspect what I'm planning—for obvious reasons."

"He would resent it?" she hazarded.

"Like hell," agreed Adam. "His vested interest demands that it's the Landell version of Watowski which gets sold to the world. He'll block us if he can." He looked at her sharply. "So I want you to be very discreet, my girl. Let me do most of the talking."

"Yes, sir," she said crisply. "Shall I wear a muzzle or a yashmak?"

Her gave her an amused, tolerant look. "You remind me of a hedgehog. All prickles and little sharp eyes..."

J.K. intervened gently. "You see, Kit, I had to lean heavily on Adam to get him to take you at all. He wanted to do the whole thing alone."

Kit bit her lip. "All right," she said after a moment, "I'll trail along in your wake, Adam." Her bright, angry green eyes said a great deal more, and Adam Rothbury had no trouble in reading their expression.

That evening, having dinner with Edward in a quiet London restaurant, she said grimly. "How am I going to put up with him day after day? I must have been mad to agree to co-operate."

"You don't seem to have had much choice," Edward said with irritating shrewdness.

She grimaced. "No. They presented me with a fait accompli, as you say. They had it all worked out. According to Sammy, they were up half the night plotting like the conspirators in a Roman tragedy."

"I suppose, to be fair, that it was Rothbury's pigeon."

"Why involve me at all, except to do the boring routine jobs? I know how it will end. I shall do most of the work, and he'll get most of the credit. It isn't fair!" She caught herself up with a groan. "Listen to me, talking like something out of a schoolgirl novel. As if life was ever fair! I must say, though, that it's time I worked with someone nice. Tom Leet followed by Rothbury is rather too much. Fate might give me a break."

"Why not ask your uncle for a transfer?"

She frowned. "I couldn't."

"Why ever not?"

"That would be taking advantage of our special relationship. Don't you see?"

"Frankly, no. Everyone knows he is your uncle. They expect him to be interested in your career. As you say, this isn't a very fair world. People realise that."

"I don't care what people think," said Kit. "My own opinion is all I care about—and I would hate myself if I used my relationship with Uncle to better my position at work. Any promotion I get will be deserved. I want to use the same ladder everybody else does, and climb at my own pace."

Edward smiled and shook his head. "You're still rather sweet and naïve, Katherine."

"Naïve?" She frowned. "Do you really think it's naïve to have integrity, Edward?"

He looked amused. "A loaded question, put like that, my dear. Of course that isn't how I see it. It's not how it is! But you have to realise how the world works. It isn't what you are, it's who you know that matters, and with an ace like J.K. up your sleeve you're ahead of the field..."

She sighed. "We shall never agree, shall we?"

"We can agree to differ," Edward said diplomatically.

She grinned at him. "No wonder you earn so much! Not only do you have that smooth-talking, solid citizen image—you have no scruples to get in your way. You look so respectable, but you're totally amoral, aren't you, Edward?"

He looked quite shocked. "Amoral? Certainly not. I firmly believe in the moral values of modern society.

"Which, according to you, don't amount to a row of beans," she pointed out.

Edward lit a cigarette. "My dear girl, you will proceed to extremes. Shall we change the subject? Tell me about this Polish poet."

"I know very little about him. I've told you most of it already. I read a few of his poems tonight. They were in a thin little volume called *The Heron Lake*. He called himself the Heron. It appears to be a play on words. Apparently he came from a village in Poland which can be translated as Heron Lake but which really meant something else which sounds just the same...a sort of double meaning. Watowski had that sort of mind."

"Did he write in English? I thought you said he was only here for two years."

"He was, but apparently he'd had an English governess, and spoke very good English before he got here."

"A governess? He sounds as if he had a wealthy background."

She nodded. "It doesn't sound as if he was a coal-miner, does it? Landell talked airily about him being an aristocrat, but he didn't give too many details. I suspect he didn't know many."

"You've looked through the Landell book on him?"

"I read the first chapter. It was more about Poland in general than Watowski in particular. There was a lot about the brave, gallant noblemen and the jolly, laughing peasants...it was written during the war, don't forget, when people still saw the world in such terms..."

"Landell is quite a famous critic," Edward observed.

"According to Adam, he built his reputation on Watowski's dead body."

"We all tend to build on other people's lives," said Edward. "Look at me—I've used my father's reputation to further my own career. People trust me because they know I'm his son."

"We're back to J.K. again," she said teasingly.

"No," Edward demurred. "You know my opinion. I won't press you further. I only say that if I were you I would use J.K. as a natural springboard. You know you're talented, but there are hundreds of talented people in television..."

"Thousands," she interrupted.

"All right, thousands! Only a few get to the top. There isn't room for more than a few. If you want to be one of the few at the top, you have to use any and every weapon you've got. Talent, contracts, personality..."

"Sex?" she asked ironically.

Edward met her direct gaze and paused frowning. Kit grinned provocatively. Edward eyed her without speaking for a moment, then said, "If I thought you meant that question seriously, I would answer it, but as I know you're just teasing, I shall ignore it."

"That is called evading the issue," she said solemnly. "You did say every weapon I had. In big business sex is a pretty powerful weapon."

"True," he agreed. "So why not try vamping Adam Rothbury for a start?"

She laughed. "You're joking! I'd rather vamp Dracula."

"Your passion for puns can be very irritating," Edward said unsmilingly. He stood up, signed the bill the waiter brought him and waited while Kit scrambled to her feet. She saw that she had offended him somehow. She never knew just where Edward would draw the line.

When she was alone in her flat that evening she sat staring at herself in the mirror. She had changed into a smooth silk nightdress, a straight-cut creation without sleeves which clung where it touched, giving her a willowy grace as she moved. The pale green shade suited her admirably, and she eyed herself thoughtfully.

Vamp Adam Rothbury? What a terrifying idea! A picture of him flashed into her mind, the lean male body stretched out casually in the deck chair on her uncle's lawn, the sunglasses hiding Adam's mocking expression while leaving the powerful jaw and firm mouth visible.

She moved restlessly, her cheeks oddly hot. Possibly some girls would find him physically attractive.

"Not me," she murmured aloud. "I've never found him attractive. And I never shall."

CHAPTER TWO

On the following Wednesday Adam picked Kit up at her flat at eleven o'clock. The weather had set fair. London was sleepy under a blue June sky, and the plane trees barely moved their green branches. Kit's flat occupied the rear ground floor of a tall Victorian house in Chelsea, a brief walk away from the grey Thames. Geraniums in white baskets made the house front gay and summery.

"A charming place to live," Adam murmured drily as he handed her into his car.

"I like it," she agreed warily.

He moved slowly away from the kerb and slotted into the lines of cars moving back into the West End. She leaned back and watched his profile, the strong jaw and powerful sweep of cheekbones and nose. The sun had touched his skin with a faint flush over the bronze of earlier weeks. He was wearing a pale blue shirt, open at the neck, and dark trousers. His jacket was slung on the back seat. It was too warm to wear it today.

"Have you met Landell before?" she asked.

"I've seen him a couple of times at parties. He socialises a good deal."

"I read his biography of Watowski."

He glanced sideways at her, one dark brow lifting. "And?"

"Very readable," she evaded.

"But?" he probed shrewdly.

She grimaced. "Too much padding. He didn't really know much about him, did he? It read like an attempt to build him up into a Polish Rupert Brooke."

"My own impression exactly," agreed Adam. "Odd!"

"Odd?" She was puzzled.

"That we should actually agree about something," he said in a silky tone.

Kit flushed. Sarcastic beast, she thought, staring straight ahead of her.

"When Landell heard that I was thinking of doing this programme he got us an invitation to the Hilton lunch. He suggested we might like to have some film of it in the programme."

"And shall you?" she asked, knowing better than to make some unsolicited comment. His biting tongue could sting unbearably.

"It sounds a good idea. My secretary fixed up something. Joe Palmer will be covering it for us." He gave her a brief grin.

Kit had smiled involuntarily at the mention of her favourite cameraman. She got on very well with Joe. A slight, wiry young man with rough fair hair and a tolerant, melancholy smile, he was good fun off duty, and brilliant at his job when he was working. He was still young enough to adore the tools of his trade. His favourite topic of conversation was cameras and the bits and pieces which came with them. He had taught her a good deal in an easy, informal fashion.

"I thought that would please you," Adam drawled.

"Joe is a friend of mine," she admitted.

"Friend?" The question was delicately mocking.

She was very pink. "Yes," she repeated defiantly. "A friend."

"Purely platonic, of course," he murmured sardonically.

"Don't you believe in platonic relationships?"

"Between a man and a woman? No. They're usually the cover for a repressed love affair."

"You do see things in crude terms, don't you?" She was angry at his tone.

"I speak from experience," he said. "I'm older than you are, remember."

"Oh, much older," she agreed, tongue in cheek. "But age doesn't necessarily equate with wisdom."

"Prickles again? Have you ever asked yourself why your prickles come out whenever you see me?" he asked, his gaze flicking over the traffic ahead.

She froze. "Perhaps because you irritate me," she retorted. "You tend to talk to me like a headmaster talking to a naughty little girl."

"If I do it's because you amuse me," he said calmly.

"I've noticed!"

"Maybe if you didn't constantly react like a naughty child I wouldn't have to treat you as one," he pointed out.

"If you didn't treat me like one I might not react as I do," she said quickly.

"We do seem to be fixed in a vicious circle, don't we?" he said.

They swung into an elegant cul-de-sac of little Georgian mews houses, bumping over the cobbles at a very low speed until they reached one with a discreet olive green door embellished with a well-polished brass lion's head knocker. A brass plate carried the name Saxton Landell.

Adam parked and turned, his arm along the wheel, to scrutinise her coolly.

"Isn't it time we broke out of our vicious circle and began to deal with each other in an adult fashion?" he asked softly.

Kit could not meet his gaze after the first moment, and lowered her eyes to her hands, linked together in the lap of her cream skirt. She was aware of a peculiar sensation, a mixture of burning heat and breathlessness, which was similar to the feeling she had had once before, just before she fainted on a hot summer day.

Huskily, she said, "I suppose so."

He was silent for a while, watching her fingers knitting restlessly together. Then he leaned over and gently separated them.

"Don't look so terrified. All I'm suggesting is a truce."

"Platonic friendship?" She could not resist the teasing question. It slipped out before she knew what she was going to say, and Adam laughed softly.

She looked up, met the amused grey eyes and looked away again, hot-cheeked.

"You already know my view on that," he returned. He lifted one of her hands. Astonished, she watched as he gently touched his lips to her wrist, his smooth dark head bent over her fingers.

Too breathless to speak, she felt him release her and turn to get out of the car. He came round, helped her out and then moved towards the front door of Landell's house. Kit followed, her heart still thudding.

Adam was already knocking. Within a moment the door had opened, and a tall, white-haired man stood there, smiling at them with conscious charm.

"Ah, here you are!"

"Not late, are we?" asked Adam, glancing at his wristwatch.

"No, no. Exactly on time. Do come in, both of you." Landell looked past him at Kit, enquiringly. "You brought your secretary?"

"This is Katherine Ashley," Adam introduced curtly.

"Ashley? Any relation of..."

"J.K.'s niece," admitted Adam, his face expressionless.

Saxton Landell held out a pale, still shapely hand towards her. He had very pale blue eyes to which his smile did not reach. They held a cold appraisal as he shook her hand.

"So you are part of your uncle's organization? That must be very exciting for you. A fascinating world, television! Do you work with Mr. Rothbury?"

"Yes, she works for me," Adam said.

Landell's gaze flicked to him. "Ah," he murmured softly. "Well, come along in and have some coffee. Or perhaps you would like some pre-luncheon sherry?"

"Coffee would be very acceptable," Adam said. "We mustn't cloud the issue, must we?"

Again the cold blue eyes flicked towards him. "No, indeed," Landell agreed warily.

He ushered them into a long, low room furnished with taste and quiet luxury. The carpet was deep-piled,

white with sprays of faded flowers. There was a cush-
ion-piled pale blue brocade sofa at one end of the
room, with matching armchairs arranged near by; at
the other end a highly-polished Georgian dining table
stood beside an open french window. The fragrance of
June roses flowed through the room.

Books lined one wall. A stereo unit took up part of
another. Landell went towards a small cupboard and
poured himself a sherry. "Coffee is already made," he
said. "You will excuse me if I don't join you? I've already had mine." He returned, gesturing for them to
sit down on the sofa. "Black or white, Miss Ashley?"

"White, thank you," she said.

He poured the coffee, then glanced at Adam, who
said quietly, "Black for me," and accepted his cup
with a nod.

Landell seated himself on a slight gilt chair, sitting
very upright, his sherry in his thin hand. He smiled at
them, sipped the sherry and waited.

Kit was fascinated. She sensed an undercurrent of
hostility between the two men. Somehow Landell had
latched on to Adam's doubts about his version of
Watowski's life, or else the critic merely disliked Adam
personally.

Adam was a past master of this sort of guarded interview. Like a cat playing with a mouse he, too,
waited, sipping his coffee and watching Landell over
the rim of the cup.

One of them had to give way. Kit knew that it was
this first silent struggle which would decide the way the
interview went.

In the event, it proved to be Landell who could not
maintain the silence.

He fiddled with his sherry glass, twisting the stem restlessly between his thin pale fingers, then said, "So you're taking over the World War Two Writers series? I thought Mr. Somerby had already done all the research he needed for the Watowski programme."

"He had completed a skeleton outline of the script," agreed Adam.

"But you're not satisfied with it?" Landell probed.

Adam watched him. "If I do a programme it has to be all mine," he drawled.

Landell laughed self-consciously. "Ah, the possessive instinct! A male characteristic, eh, Miss Ashley?"

Kit met his gaze with a start, then felt herself beginning to flush. She guessed that he had seen Adam kiss her wrist as they sat in the car. No doubt he had been watching from the window for their arrival.

Landell looked pleased with himself. He glanced at Adam, to test his reaction, but Adam was poker-faced.

Instead he rose and crossed the room to look at a framed pen-and-ink sketch hanging opposite the bookcases. Landell watched him. Adam turned. "Watowski," he said, in statement rather than question.

"No doubt you recognise it," said Landell. "It's the sketch I used as the frontispiece for my book."

"Who did it?"

"Oh, a friend of his, not an artist, as you see, but the likeness is oddly good. He was a very handsome young man."

Kit joined Adam. She, too, recognised the sketch. Watowski was in profile, his hair swept back by an invisible wind from a high, bony forehead, his features lightly sketched in with a few faint strokes. It was, as Landell had said, a handsome face, with a wild recklessness which came through even in this amateur sketch.

"Such a pity he died so young." Landell murmured. "So much genius expunged in a moment. He might have been another Keats."

"How many times did you actually meet him?" Adam asked directly.

Landell paused, his face wary. "Well, that's a poser," he said after a moment, his smile tight. "So long ago, of course. Old men forget, you know. Does it matter? It's not how long we knew each other, surely, but how well?"

"And how well did you know him?" Adam pressed.

"After one hour's conversation, I think, anyone with a soul would have known that this was a young man destined for greatness," Landell mused dreamily.

"Where did you meet him, by the way?" Adam asked casually, sauntering along the bookcase and eyeing the rows of beautifully bound books.

"At one of those casual, wartime parties," said the older man.

Adam paused, took down a leather-bound edition of the Shakespearean Sonnets and flipped over the pages. "What an exquisite edition," he admired aloud. "I envy you your books, Mr. Landell. They must be the result of a lifetime's collecting."

Landell relaxed slightly, smiled tolerantly. "Oh, certainly. My hobby and my weakness, I'm afraid. It costs a fortune to have a book bound in leather these days. I've just had my copy of *Persuasion* rebound. It cost me fifteen pounds, believe it or not. Quite incredible.''

"Good heavens!'' exclaimed Adam. "Beyond the range of my pocket, I'm afraid.''

Landell relaxed even further. "You will come to it, my dear boy, one of these days. I'm sure you're going to set the Thames on fire.''

"Oh, I doubt if I'm destined for greatness,'' Adam said drily.

Landell laughed indulgently. "Well, perhaps not quite that, but I've heard they pay very well in television. You must get Miss Ashley's uncle to give you a raise.''

Adam smiled politely. "Who gave the party, did you say?'' He asked the question so suddenly that Landell was thrown off balance. Lulled into a sense of false security by Adam's flattery, he had forgotten to be on his guard. Now he stammered, looking taken aback.

"Oh...er...Theodor Poniatowski, I think. Another Pole, of course. A Count, if you can believe him. He flew with Jan, knew him slightly. But Theo was not in the same class as Jan. Purely materialistic—no soul.''

"Theodor Poniatowski?'' Adam's brow wrinkled. "Isn't he the chap who runs Theo's Bistro in Knightsbridge? I always thought he was a Russian, somehow.''

Landell walked to the french window and stood, half turned away from them, staring into the garden. His voice had an irritable ring. "Yes, that's Theo. I'm afraid he won't be much use to you. He hates to be reminded of the old days. He lives for the profit motive. He has three restaurants, scattered all over London, coining money for him."

Adam nodded. "I've eaten at one or two of them. The food is good, but the prices are a bit steep."

"Indeed they are," agreed Landell, returning, his face smoothed out in a cold smile. "And now I come to think of it I believe he's in Paris at the moment, opening a restaurant over there."

"That's right. I saw something about it in the papers," Adam nodded. "Oh, well, it doesn't matter. Tell me about Watowski. How did you learn that he was a poet?"

"I was editing a magazine at the time I met him. I called it *Flamebearer*." Landell looked at him questioningly. "You may have heard of it."

"Who hasn't?" Adam smiled. "You introduced a great deal of exciting new writing to the public, didn't you?"

"Well, I would like to believe so," Landell sighed. "Such a vast amount of it made no impression. Like pouring water into sand. Quite depressing at times."

"But Watowski sent some poems to you?"

"Yes. After I had met him at this party he sent me some poems. They were startlingly original, and I printed several in *Flamebearer*. He sent me a sheaf of them afterwards. Before I had had time to print any more, however, he was killed in action. Tragic, quite tragic."

"But you had the poems," Adam commented.

Kit watched Landell closely. She saw a curious flicker pass over the smooth face. Landell looked at Adam with smiling hostility.

"When I read them through again I knew that it was my duty to see that they survived, even though that poor boy had not. I managed to persuade Grant & Yates to bring them out." He spread his hands in a charming shrug. "It was uphill work, but at last they agreed. It was wonderful to feel that I had played some small part in bringing his work before the public."

"A very large part, I would say," Adam said.

Landell demurred modestly, "No, no. I only did what I knew had to be done."

"And who was the girl?" Adam asked suddenly.

Again, Landell was thrown. He laughed nervously. "Well, who can be certain? With a boy as handsome as that? It could have been one of a dozen pretty creatures. He always had a crowd around him. He was like the sun, he shone forth and the flowers lifted their faces to him adoringly."

"Quite," said Adam smoothly. He held out his hand. "Well, it's been very kind of you to spare us so much of your valuable time. I'm very grateful."

Landell looked astonished. "Is that all?" He smiled nervously. "I mean, have I answered all your questions?"

"Oh, I think Harry's script told me most of what I wanted to know," Adam shrugged. "I just wanted to dot the i's and cross the t's, you know. It's an awkward business taking over another man's programme. I felt I had to talk to you at first hand. One mustn't take anything on trust in the television world."

"Oh, of course," said Landell eagerly. His air of relief was blatant. He ushered them to the door, talking fulsomely, and shook hands before they left.

"We'll be in touch when we want you to come in to the studio," Adam told him.

"Of course, you'll want to get this on film," nodded Landell. "How soon do you think...?"

"A matter of weeks," said Adam. "I'm still tying up loose ends on another programme, I'm afraid."

"And shall we see you at the Hilton lunch?"

"I'll be there," Adam said.

Landell gave Kit a little parting smile. She smiled back, but was glad to be leaving. There was something about him which made her uneasy. He was too smooth, too polite. Beneath that pleasant exterior lurked something far less pleasant.

As they drove away Adam asked her idly, "What did you make of him?"

"Slippery," she said.

Adam laughed. "Shrewd of you. Yes, he was, wasn't he?"

"You pressed him rather hard. He guessed you were after him," she said.

He nodded. "Yes, that was deliberate. From the moment we arrived I knew Landell was going to be difficult. I had to choose between spending weeks lulling him into losing his suspicion of me, or going for a head-on attack."

"So you tried a mixture of both," she said. "You kept changing your attitude—I noticed that. At the end he wasn't sure how you felt about anything."

"I hope you're right," he said. "What I don't want is to have Landell muddying the waters before I can start fishing in them."

"In what way?"

"He might nobble a few people," Adam said casually.

"Like Theodor Poniatowski?"

"Like him," agreed Adam.

"But he's in Paris, anyway."

"There are regular flights to Paris."

Kit stared at him. "You're really going to chase over there to interview Poniatowski?"

"I'm on holiday. I can please myself. J.K. can pay for my trip though, so I'll get a visit to Paris on expenses, all legitimate."

She was silent, envying him. The traffic was thickening for the lunch break and the air reeked of petrol fumes.

They swept along beside St. James's Park. The lawns were crowded with sunbathers, stretched out on the grass to enjoy the beneficent sun, the men barechested, the women in sleeveless blouses. The trees stood in dark seas of shade and the ducks squawked loudly as a woman in a cotton dress threw bread to them. They were forced to halt suddenly as a mother duck decided to shepherd her little brood across the road for a cooling dip in the lake. Kit laughed, delighted, as the little procession quacked and waddled past. A line of cars drew up patiently behind them. Londoners were accustomed to such incidents.

Outside Buckingham Palace the crowds drifted desultorily, talking and taking photographs of the redcoated soldiers. Across the tarmacked forecourt the blank windows of the Palace reflected back the sun. The Royal Standard floated above the roof. The Queen was in residence for her birthday celebrations.

"I've never seen the Trooping the Colour except on television," Kit said suddenly.

"How typical of a Londoner," Adam smiled. "People come from all corners of the world to see things like that, yet Londoners often live in the capital for fity years without bothering to take the trouble."

"I suppose we only value what we know is out of reach," she said. "If I was a visitor to London I'd make sure I saw it, but every year I say to myself, oh, well, some other time I'll get to see it. There always seems to be a good reason why I don't go. All those crowds, for one thing."

"Have you seen the Queen's Gallery? She has some superb pictures on exhibition, well worth a visit."

Kit grimaced. "Not yet. I did go to Windsor last summer. I did all the tourist things, walked along the Long Walk through the Park to the Copper Horse."

"George III, you mean," Adam corrected. "Someone once called it the Copper Horse to Queen Victoria, and she drew herself up to her full height and said icily, 'My lord, that is not a Copper Horse, that is my grandfather.'"

Kit laughed. "I can imagine it! It's a marvellous statue, a lovely greeny colour, poised on a stone plinth. The horse really is amazingly well done. It paws the air in a very lifelike way, on its hind legs as if it was about to leap off the plinth and gallop off."

They drew up at a canopied restaurant in a shady street. The bustle and hubbub of London seemed suddenly miles away.

"I thought we would have lunch and talk about our trip to Paris," said Adam, getting out.

Kit's pulses leapt as he helped her out of the car. "*Our* trip to Paris?"

"This is a joint venture," he reminded her.

"Yes, but..."

"Do you imagine J.K. will disapprove of you accompanying me to Paris?"

"Of course not," she said indignantly. "I often go away with Edward."

"Ah," drawled Adam. "Your smooth-suited friend?"

She flushed. "Edward Montague," she expanded coldly. "He's an architect."

"And you suspect he won't approve of Paris, is that it?"

"I don't intend to ask him," she snapped. "I'm not anyone's property."

Adam's brow quirked upward mockingly. "Not another platonic friendship, surely?"

"No," she said recklessly. "Not a bit platonic."

"So," murmured Adam very silkily. "Interesting."

His hand was beneath her elbow, and Kit found herself moving into the restaurant. Small, clipped bay trees in white pots stood on either side of the door, and inside it was cool and quiet. Venetian blinds kept the sun out and air-conditioning maintained an even temperature.

Adam had booked a table, she found. Moments later, they were seated in an alcove studying the vast menu. Kit ordered melon and steak, and Adam did the same. The waiter hovered discreetly, poured a little wine into Adam's glass and waited until he had nodded before filling their glasses.

As they ate their melon Adam asked her, "Your passport is in order, I presume?"

"Yes," she nodded.

"Are you free to leave on Friday? No loose ends to be tied up before you leave?"

"That depends on how long we're going to be away," she said.

"We'll probably come back on Monday," he said. "We might as well make a weekend of it." He surveyed her briefly with a wry glint in his grey eyes. "Unless you object."

She shrugged with pretended nonchalance. "Why not? It will be wonderful to be in Paris in this weather."

"Do you know it well?"

"I've been there several times."

"And liked it?"

"Who could dislike Paris?"

"I know people who do."

"I know people who dislike Shakespeare," she said. "I violently disapprove of their taste, however."

He laughed. "Well, we all have our blind spots." Slyly, he added, "You have often exhibited symptoms of disliking me."

She choked on her spoonful of melon.

Adam laughed again. "Well, we've signed our truce, haven't we? Signed and sealed with a kiss, as you might say."

She glared at him. "Landell saw that."

He grinned. "Yes, I suspected he had, too. He obviously felt that he'd learnt something useful about us—he probably thinks you're my mistress."

She went red. "I hope he doesn't."

Adam eyed her. "You do change colour easily. I think you must have some chameleon blood."

"At least my blood is red," she snapped.

He lifted an eyebrow. "What on earth is that supposed to mean? That mine isn't?"

"You have a reputation for bloodlessness," she said. "Don't say you didn't know!"

"Am I omniscient, too, then?"

"You're..." The words choked in her throat and she broke off without finishing her sentence.

He looked mockingly at her. "Yes? Go on! I can almost see the adjectives jamming up on your tongue..."

She bit her lip as the waiter advanced once more to remove their plates. With difficulty she sipped her wine. The waiter deftly replenished her glass at once, and she gave him a very small smile.

When he had vanished once again she looked at Adam directly. "What happened to our truce?"

"We do seem to start skirmishing rather easily, don't we?" Adam smiled. "These platonic relationships are obviously fraught with unknown dangers."

"Do you have to keep harping on platonic relationships?" she snapped.

"I thought you preferred them?"

"Well, I don't," she said, abandoning dignity. "And I wish you would shut up about them."

"Ah, yes," he said. "I'd forgotten—there's the charming Edward. Is it serious between you?"

"Is that any business of yours?"

"I was only showing polite interest," he complained sadly. "If we're to work together, especially while we're in Paris for the weekend, we ought to know how things stand."

"I prefer to keep business and pleasure apart," she said.

"And which am I?" he enquired. "Which category would you put me in?"

The waiter arrived with their steak, and Kit waited until he had gone once more before replying. "You come under the category of Crosses to be Borne," she said. "You seem determined to torment the life out of me, I can't think why."

Adam surveyed her silently, his grey eyes briefly grave. "Do you know, neither can I," he said after a moment.

She felt a frisson of alarm down her spine. Hurriedly she turned her attention to her steak. It was superbly cooked, and the salad served with it was crisp and fresh, delicately flavoured with oil, lemon and herbs. For a while they ate in silence, then Adam said softly, "I have a strange suspicion that there's a lot behind this Watowski business. There's no evidence to prove it, but I have a very strong hunch, and I always follow my hunches." He looked up at her, his mouth mocking. "I have a hunch about you, too, Katherine Mary Ashley."

She held her breath, waiting for him to go on, and after a moment, he did, adding, "But I'm not going to tell you what it is yet. Timing is everything, as my first boss in television taught me."

CHAPTER THREE

PARIS in June smells of horse-chestnut blossom. The great white candles of flowers light the blue sky and send incense-like clouds of fragrance drifting across the city. The steel-grey Seine twists under its bridges and throws back images of the sky, fretted by towers and spires of the earth-bound city.

Adam had somehow managed to book them into a central hotel, a magical feat at this time of year when Paris is crammed with tourists. They whirred up to their rooms in a small green lift. The corridor was silent, carpeted, smelling of polish and summer dust.

Adam and Kit separated at her door. He was in a room facing hers, she saw.

Alone in the box-like room, she unpacked her small yellow leather case. She had brought the bare minimum of clothes. She shook out a black chiffon evening dress, a short drift of fragile material which would, she saw, need pressing before it could be worn. She had also brought two blouses, a sweater and a pleated white skirt. She wanted to be prepared for any occasion.

Later, she took a shower in the bathroom adjacent to her own room. Wrapped in a long, transparent cotton gown, she perched on her bed, afterwards attending to her toes. When someone knocked on the door it made her jump.

"Come in," she called.

Adam came in and stared at her with lifted eyebrows. "Not ready? I thought we'd have a stroll before dinner."

"Can you give me ten minutes?" she asked, popping the top back on to her nail varnish bottle.

Adam looked sceptical. "Ten minutes? If you're like most women that means an hour..."

"Ten minutes," she repeated. "Close the door as you go out, please."

He sighed. "O.K. Then I'll be back in ten minutes."

In fact, Kit was ready just as he knocked again, and she enjoyed the surprise on his face when she joined him, her black chiffon dress swirling silkily around her slender legs.

"You never cease to astonish me," he admitted frankly. "Aren't you going to wear a jacket?"

She picked up a fine-meshed silvery shawl from the bed. "I shall wear this."

"Will it be warm enough?"

"Why not? It is June, remember."

"Even in Paris the weather can turn cold, especially at night."

"It'll be all right. I'm warm-blooded."

A mocking glint came into the grey eyes. "Are you indeed? That's interesting. We must see if you're right, mustn't we?"

Her heart thudding, she preceded him into the corridor, her shawl loosely draped around her arms and shoulders. She was not sure whether she preferred

Adam in his new role as charming flirt. At least she had known where she was when he behaved like Attila the Hun in the office. Now her reactions were confused and contradictory. She no longer knew how she felt towards him, especially since, having seen him at work coaxing and bullying interviewees, she was perfectly well aware that a cold, analytical brain controlled his behaviour, however impulsive it might seem to those who did not know him. If Adam was being charming to her it only meant that he had decided to make her malleable. He might have any of a dozen reasons for wishing her to like him.

They emerged into the still sunlit streets and wandered idly through the busy heart of Paris, shop-window gazing, pausing to watch a girl change a display of hats in an exclusive milliner's window. The girl caught Adam's eye, and, flirtatious Parisienne as she was, pouted enquiringly as she twirled a tiny concoction of lace and straw upon one finger. Adam made a gesture of ravishment, smiled with male appreciation, let his grey eyes admiringly flick over the girl's slight figure in skintight blue jeans and T-shirt. The girl laughed, pleased. Kit walked on, aware of a curious little constriction in her throat.

Adam caught up with her. His expression was amused. "By the way, I've booked a table at the new Bistro," he said.

"The one Theodor Poniatowski is opening here?"

"It opened last night. I spoke to Poniatowski himself. He'll join us for a drink after we've eaten. He promised me the best meal in Paris."

"Do you think Landell has been in touch with him?"

"No," Adam said, "I don't think he has."

They walked down to the Seine, leaned on the parapet and stared into the water. Twilight was falling, giving a pale lavender wash to the sky. Barges on the river bobbed slightly to and fro, covered by draped tarpaulins. The lights came on in a sleek cruiser on the far side. They were reflected in the grey waters. An illuminated river boat passed slowly, and they faintly heard the megaphoned voice of the guide describing Paris to the passengers.

Kit was strongly aware of Adam's elbow touching hers, his sleeve against her arm.

He turned his head suddenly and looked into her eyes. "You look pensive," he said lightly. "That isn't allowed in Paris. Smile, come on . . ."

She could not do it. A strange, troubling melancholy had descended upon her spirits, a restless sadness she did not understand.

He put a finger under her chin, raised her face and looked at her more closely. "The spell is potent, isn't it?"

"What spell?" she asked vaguely.

"Paris," he murmured. "Can't you feel it in the river breeze, hear it in the sighing of the trees, see it in the lights across the river? This is the city of romance, the city of lovers." He bent slowly forward. Kit watched his face with a trance-like expectation. When his lips touched hers, her eyelids closed and her hands went up to cling to his shoulders. The kiss was brief, gentle, coaxing. It left her aroused but unsatisfied.

Adam withdrew. He smiled at her gravely. "I'm hungry," he said in a calm voice. "Let's go."

They took a taxi to the new Bistro. Kit angrily admonished herself as they drove through the crowded streets. What was the matter with her? Why was she letting Adam manipulate her as if she was a puppet? Of course he was playing some game, he did not have any serious interest in her, yet as soon as he turned the famous Rothbury charm upon her she crumbled like dust before him. Have some self-respect, she told herself. Next time he turns on the charm, slap his face!

Long before she met him she had heard about his women. He was usually seen in public with exquisite, model-like creatures with sleek hair and beautiful clothes. They changed as often as his mood, it appeared, but in one thing they were constant—they were all ravishing.

I'm not beautiful, Kit thought crossly. I bear no resemblance at all to a model. He can't be interested in me. He's just playing some devious game.

Could it be that this tough, ambitious man was using her as a weapon in his climb to the top? She was J.K.'s niece, after all, and although she was determined never to use her position to get on, she knew that other ambitious men had seen her as a valuable pawn. She had quickly learnt to recognise the flatterers who clustered around J.K. and paid her eager attention. One reason for her reluctant admiration for Adam had been his harshness towards her from the first. She had been certain of his integrity, however much she resented his tough treatment.

The Bistro was situated in a back street of Montmartre. The narrow, eighteenth-century house in which it was housed was newly painted white. Shut-

ters outlined the windows. A black cat prowled around
the entrance, a bell tinkling on its neck.

Lights streamed from the windows on the ground
floor. The discreet sound of taped music met them as
they entered. Little tables with frilled Victorian lamps
placed centrally on them; ferns in great china pots; red
plush and deep carpets, English wallpaper.

Standing near the door was a gigantic figure in full
evening dress, a scarlet-lined evening cloak loose from
his shoulders. Black hair curled riotously on his leon-
ine head. The threads of silver among the black had
been left to add distinction, and black moustaches
made a thick bar above a full pink mouth.

He glanced at them as they entered. Adam smiled
and held out a hand. "Count Poniatowski? I'm Adam
Rothbury, and this is my assistant, Kit Ashley."

"My dear fellow," boomed the Count, shaking
their hands. "And welcome, Miss Ashley...Kit? What
is this Kit? But it suits you. You look like a ginger kitten. Do you have sharp claws? If I were younger what
fun to find out!" He lifted her hand and kissed it,
bowing gallantly. "You have beautiful hands, Miss
Kit, white and delicate. Your nails are not ruined by
typewriting."

"Beware my dear Count," Adam drawled, watching them impassively. "As you say, they're sharp little claws . . ."

The Count's dark eyes twinkled from Adam to Kit.
"So? Young men experiment dangerously still, I see."

Kit felt herself blushing.

"All life is experience," Adam said.

The Count laughed. "One day I will tell you of my
experiences, my dear fellow." He had a ripe English

public school accent only faintly tinged with an East European lilt, the mixture making him dangerously charming. Kit could well imagine that he must have been a very attractive young man.

"Now first you will eat. Tonight I serve veal, in a sauce which is almost too beautiful to eat. You will enjoy this. I have ordered for you. Please to be seated and the waiters will attend to you. Later I will join you." He smiled, bowed and then darted away to greet some new arrivals. They heard his charming compliments showering down upon the feminine members of the little party, who smiled delightedly and preened themselves.

The menu was chalked on a large blackboard displayed by the kitchen door. There was no choice of meals. The Bistro served one main course only. There were only a dozen tables, and the service, as they soon discovered, was leisurely. It was expected that you would take your time.

They were presented with oysters, which Kit eyed with deep misgiving. "I don't like them," she whispered to Adam.

"Have you ever eaten them?"

"No," she admitted. "I don't like the thought of them."

"Try them," he advised.

Reluctantly, she raised one to her lips and imitated the motion with which he slid the oyster down his throat. It made her shiver with distaste, however, and she refused to eat any more. The waiter deftly removed her plate and whisked away with it, returning in a moment with an hors d'oeuvres trolley. Gratefully, she chose a selection and ate them while Adam finished the oysters. They were drinking champagne from a bottle which Adam scrutinised with respect.

"This is first class," he commented.

"It is on the house, m'sieur," the waiter told him. "Compliments of Count Theo..."

"Very kind of him," Adam smiled.

The veal arrived, paper-thin slivers of meat in a delicate sauce with Pommes Anna and spears of broccoli.

"It isn't surprising that his restaurants do so well," Kit sighed, refusing a sweet. "His cook is superb."

They were drinking black coffee and nibbling slices of fresh orange when Count Theo joined them, his black eyes flattering Kit as he chose to sit beside her.

They complimented him on the meal, and he shrugged and smiled. "I am pleased you enjoyed it." His black eyes twinkled at her. "Even though you do not love oysters!"

She laughed. "I'm afraid I can never see the point of them—they're gone in a second and they taste like wet plastic..."

"Heresy!" he mocked her gently. "I see you need educating, little kitten. How I would enjoy taking you in hand! With hair like yours you would be a rewarding pupil."

She looked at him from beneath her lashes, her smile provocative. "What a pity I'm only in Paris for a weekend!"

He looked enchanted. "But even in two days Paris can work miracles! And I am a superb teacher."

"I think you are a dangerous man, Count," she told him. "I would soon be out of my depth."

"But how enjoyable you would find it! One can drown so exquisitely in those waters!"

She laughed. "Don't tempt me!"

"Perhaps we could get down to business if you two have finished flirting so blatantly," Adam said crisply.

The Count glanced across the table at him, his black eyes shrewd. "Ah, am I invading private territory, my dear fellow? You must forgive me. Miss Kitten is so enchantingly young, and I have reached the stage at which youth has a charm beyond anything else life has to offer."

Adam smiled tightly at him. "We never value youth until we've lost it for ever," he said. "Jan Watowski wrote a sonnet about being young. Do you remember it?"

The Count shrugged. "Me, I do not read much poetry. I have no time—I am too busy building an empire." His grin was self-derisory. "But you want to talk about my friend Jan. I loved him." The words were deep and sincere. "We fought together, laughed together, loved together. We shared women and wine, death and victory. Then he paid the price, but I survived. He is part of my youth, part of myself. What can I tell you about him that Landell has not told the world?"

"You've read Landell's book?"

"I read the first chapter." The Count grimaced. "As I said, I have no time for such things as reading. And the part I read was boring."

"Was it accurate, though?" Adam pressed.

The Count grimaced again. "All that stuff about Poland? No, of course not. Pure rubbish. What can such a man know about Poland? Has he ever been there? Has he lived there, felt the heartbeat of the country? He talks like a Hollywood film from the days before the war. Only a Pole can speak of Poland with truth."

"How well did Landell know Jan?"

The Count laughed. "Hardly at all. I introduced them at a party. When Jan heard that Landell edited some obscure magazine he was eager to sell him poems. Landell published some of them, but when Jan sent him more, we heard nothing of them. It was not until months later, after Jan's death, that Landell remembered the poems Jan had sent. Myself, I think he forgot about them, had no intention of publishing them, until Jan's death gave him the idea of creating a war hero poet."

Adam looked interested, leant forward. "You had that impression too, did you?"

The Count eyed him thoughtfully. "So? That is how you also see it? Now I see you are a man one can respect. I tell you this . . . Landell used Jan for his own purposes. Whether Jan's poetry was good I cannot tell, but I am sure of this much—Landell was not so very impressed until after Jan's death."

"Did they meet often after that first encounter, do you know?"

The Count shrugged. "I do not see how. Jan was flying, you know. He had little spare time, and he did not spend that in London with those gabble-merchants of the intelligentsia."

"Where did he spend his spare time?"

The Count shrugged. "Where do young men spend their days when they are laying their lives on the line night after night?"

Adam smiled. "Wine, women and song?"

"Where else? Life is short during a war. One feels the urgency to fill one's time with all the sweetness one may soon be unable to experience again. Jan and I lived fully in those short months. We drank and gambled and pursued beautiful women."

"So Landell's picture of Watowski as a dreamy young poet sitting up all night to scribble deathless lines is not altogether accurate?"

The Count laughed hugely. "Jan preferred experience of a more earthy sort."

"He did write the poems, though," Kit intervened.

The Count shrugged. "Oh, of course. He would jot them down on the backs of envelopes, on menu cards, on scraps of paper anywhere. I have seen him scribbling away in the cockpit before now. But he would never pass up the chance of a party in order to stay behind and write."

Kit had a clear vision suddenly of the young pilot, his windblown hair wildly disordered, his face intent, scribbling on the back of an envelope while he waited to take off for a duel in the English skies.

"Were there lots of girls?" she asked. "One gets the impression that there was one special one . . . the later sonnets seem to have a common theme."

The Count lifted his broad shoulders in a shrug. "There were many girls at first, but one week-end he went off to fish in the country somewhere, and from then on he used to vanish without a word during his days off, and I suspect there was someone special tucked away. He never talked about her, though, and I didn't ask. I had my own life to lead."

"So you never met her?"

"No. I have no idea who she was, or where she lived. Except that it was somewhere in the country, I suspect. This all happened in the last three months."

"And no girl ever enquired about him after his death?" Kit asked incredulously. She was sure that if she had been in love with someone she would make desperate attempts to get in touch with his friends to hear about his death.

The Count laughed suddenly. "Someone did enquire about him from our squadron leader, I remember!"

"Yes?" Adam and Kit listened intently.

"She was certainly not Jan's girl, though. She was a withered old hag of a landlady who claimed that Jan owed her money, and she wanted to be paid off. The squadron leader told her that Jan had paid with his life that she should be free, but this did not seem to impress her much."

"You don't remember anything about her that might help us to trace her?" asked Adam.

The Count scratched his chin doubtfully. "You ask the impossible, you know, after all these years. I doubt if I ever even knew her name, and even if I had I do not imagine I would remember it now. I do remember, though, that she came from a West Country village, because I gathered that the squadron leader had recommended the place to Jan as a good place to get some fishing."

"Then do you remember the name of the village?" Adam asked him eagerly.

"My dear fellow, you do expect miracles! At this distance in time? Why don't you ask the squadron leader? I suppose you will want to see him, too."

"He's still alive?"

"Very much so. I still see him from time to time. Once a year he dines at my Knightsbridge Bistro. He was my first customer when it opened, and he has remained faithful ever since."

"So he lives in London?"

"No, no, he is a farmer now. He lives in Cambridgeshire, I seem to remember—I couldn't tell you offhand. My address book is in London. But if you contact my secretary in London she will look it up for you."

"What is his name?"

"Loxford. George Loxford," said the Count. "He is a good chap, George." He grinned at them. "That is what he calls me—a good chap! English is a very strange language. Don't you agree with me, young lady?"

"You speak it very well," Kit said.

He gave her an intimate little smile. "I learnt it as I learnt everything important—from a woman! Ah, that is how to imprint things on the heart, whether you are two or seventy-two!"

Kit was amused by this man. He had such panache, such grandeur of self-assurance. He reminded her of a fairy tale character. The dull mediocrities of ordinary life were beneath him. Everything he said and did was larger than life, grandiloquent, gallant, charming.

He insisted on buying them a brandy, drank several from deep green brandy glasses, swirling the amber liquid around as he talked, his dark eyes attentive to every expression on Kit's face. Adam leaned back and watched expressionlessly, saying nothing. Having achieved the answers to his main questions he took no further part in the conversation.

Kit listened as the Count talked of his flying days, laughed at the superstitions the pilots had cherished yet which he himself had clearly been influenced by, too; remembered long-dead comrades and forgotten faces. Jan Watowski's name came easily from his lips from time to time. Kit gained a gradual picture of the young poet. She heard of him playing hopscotch in an East End street with a band of ragged children, of his bestowing his month's sweet ration upon them before he left. She heard of him reeling drunkenly along English country lanes, falling into a ditch choked with wild parsley and other country flowers, and climbing out reeking of wild garlic which he had somehow managed to crush in his fall.

"We turned him out of barracks that night," said Count Theo. "It was more than flesh and blood could stand. He had to scrub himself to get rid of the stink of it."

"At least it kept vampires away," said Kit.

The Count gave a bark of amusement. "So, you make jokes about it! You did not have to stand the smell! No wonder vampires do not like it."

Adam stood up. "We must go," he said. "Thanks for the hospitality, Count, and for your help. I'm very grateful. I'll sign the bill, if I may."

The Count made a sweeping gesture of dissent. "No bill! This time it is on the house. Next time you can pay, but tonight I am happy only to have had such charming company. I feel a young man again with those pretty green eyes gazing at me. Ah, this is how Othello felt as Desdemona listened to his tales of warfare long ago!'' He lifted Kit's hand to his mouth, kissed the palm, the fingers one by one, the wrist. ''If I were younger I would pursue you hotly,'' he told her. ''You have spirit and femininity. I do not like a girl to be too tough, eh? Modern girls frighten me. A girl should be soft and yielding, sweet as melting honey, yet with a strong core.'' He gave Adam a little flicking glance, teasingly shrewd. ''For a man this is the greatest pleasure in life—to master these fragile, tempestuous creatures. You agree, Rothbury?''

Adam gave him a cool, unreadable look. ''Perhaps.''

''Now that is English! To assent and reserve judgment at one and the same time. No wonder the French call you hypocrites. You are masters of compromise. Like your English weather you are variable, unpredictable, always moderate.'' He embraced Adam suddenly in a vast bear-hug. ''I like you,'' he said warmly. ''Come and see me in London. We will drink together.''

Emerging from the Bistro into chill night air, Kit shivered, and Adam gave her a frosty glance. ''I told you to wear something warmer than that. The temperature has dropped appreciably since we got here.''

''I'll get used to it as we walk,'' she said. ''I don't want to go back to the hotel yet. It's too early to go to bed, and I'm too excited.''

Adam ignored her, hailing a taxi with a peremptory gesture. He bundled her, protesting, into it and gave the address of their hotel. ''We'll have a last drink before we turn in, if you like,'' he conceded.

The taxi driver drove with Gallic fury, swerving between other cars, hooting fiercely, at tremendous speed. As he took a corner Kit was thrown against Adam and he caught her to steady her. The bodily contact made her suddenly breathless.

"Are you all right?" he asked.

In the darkness of the cab their eyes met. Kit had drunk more wine than she was accustomed to, and her responses were less controlled than she intended. Her drowsy, aroused expression was revealing.

Adam's hands slid down her arms, encircled her waist. She sighed and bent towards him, weak with passion.

Their lips met and clung hotly. She felt his hands moving caressingly up and down her back, arousing a hunger she had never felt before. Flinging her arms around his neck, she twisted closer, stroking his dark hair and the strong nape of his neck. His mouth was demanding an equal response to the passion he offered her, and Kit's bones seemed to melt within her. She could hardly breathe. Just when she felt she would suffocate, Adam slid his mouth from hers and began to kiss her chin, her throat, her shoulders, his face burrowing like a child below the fragile chiffon of her gown.

The taxi stopped suddenly, with a jolt, and she was shaken out of her abandonment. She sat up, very flushed, smoothing down her hair.

Adam paid the taxi driver, who grinned at them in silence, winking at Kit.

They went into the hotel, blinking at the brilliance of the lights like owls.

"Do you still want that drink?" Adam asked huskily.

She hardly dared to meet his eyes. Gazing at the floor, she shook her head.

"I...I think I'd better go straight to bed," she whispered.

They went up in silence in the little lift. At the door of her room she halted, hesitating. But Adam merely nodded to her and went into his own room without a backward glance.

She closed her door and leaned against it, breathing thickly. How could he make love to her like that, then walk away so coolly? Was that all it meant to him? A kiss in a taxi quickly forgotten? An opportunity snatched?

Hot-cheeked and angry with herself for allowing him to rouse her like that, she stumbled into the bathroom and took a cool shower. Then, in her brief cotton nightdress, a thin drift of pale green with daisies printed on it, she was about to climb into bed when there was a tap at the door. She snatched up her dressing-gown, but before she had time to slip into it the door had opened and Adam stood there.

She glared at him. "What the hell are you doing in my room at this time of night? If you have the idea I think you have, you can forget it! Get out!"

His mouth twisted ironically. He held up his thumb. Blood was pouring from it, dark red and ominous. "I cut myself on my pocket knife. Have you got a plaster?"

She was covered with embarrassed confusion. "Oh...I see. Yes, I think I have, as it happens. I always carry some in my case when I go away." She searched in the small top drawer of the dressing-table, found a little tin of plasters. As she turned away she saw herself in the mirror, a slight girl in a revealing nightdress, her cheeks bright pink, her hair damp and dishevelled. I'm hardly a sight to drive a man crazy with desire, she told herself angrily. What a fool to jump to conclusions!

She made him come into her bathroom, washed and dried the cut, gently applied the dressing.

"There, I think that will be all right," she said. "I'm sorry I...I jumped to conclusions. Stupid of me. It must be the brandy I had on top of that wine."

"You're right to be suspicious," he said calmly. "I had quite a struggle with myself when we parted. Count Theo hit the nail on the head when he said you were a temptation to any red-blooded male. That look of yielding innocence can drive men crazy, you know. It's the same impulse that makes children long to run over untrodden snow. The desire to touch, to possess what's virgin and untouched..."

Kit heard her pulses hammering, her breath coming roughly. "You're sure I am...untouched?" she asked lamely.

Adam laughed grimly. "I damned well know it. You're like a young filly who's never known the bridle. You duck and run at the first approach, yet you're possessed with curiosity about life. When I kissed you just now I knew for certain that it was all new to you. Your smooth-suited Edward has taught you nothing. The fellow must be a fool."

"Edward wasn't the first to take me out, you know," she said, stung to anger. "I've had boyfriends since I was a teenager."

"I don't doubt it. Boys of your own age, not men."

She glared at him. "Honestly, your arrogance is breathtaking! You're not a man, you're a dinosaur. Your kind should be extinct. But you plod on, believing yourself invincible, irresistible, and making colossal mistakes about everything around you..."

He laughed, his grey eyes taunting her. "I haven't made any mistake about you, Katherine Mary Ashley. I know you from your red head down to your size four feet."

"You know nothing about me," she flung furiously. "You only think you do because of your own vanity!"

"Very well," he said softly. "If you want it that way... you're an enigma and a mystery to me, but whatever you are, you're perfectly aware that you've been giving me the green light ever since we got to Paris, and I wouldn't be human if I didn't seize my chance when it was offered so enchantingly."

"Oh!" Kit felt as though he had punched her in the chest with these words. Rage burned at the back of her eyes and she looked at him with hatred. "That's a lie! I haven't been giving you any green light. I..."

Adam shrugged. "Why should we argue about it? As you seem to have changed your mind we'll just forget it, shall we? There are plenty of other fish in the sea."

"That applies to both of us," she snapped.

He gave her a chilly little smile. "Naturally. You find yourself some nice polite boy, and I'll find myself a real woman, one who knows the truth about her own feelings and how to enjoy an adult life. We wouldn't want any violent emotions to make an untidy mess of your neat little existence, would we, even if it means you remain a frozen spinster for the rest of your life?''

''I won't do that, thanks,'' she said bitterly. ''I'll meet a man I can fall in love with and marry. Most girls do. Until then, I'll make sure I don't ruin my peace of mind with messy experiments like the one you were apparently proposing for us.''

His mouth twisted. ''Yes, love is a messy experiment, Kit. It's like a time bomb. Sooner or later it goes off and blows your life to pieces.''

The door closed behind him quietly. Kit stared at it without seeing anything but his shuttered face as he said the last words. She felt shaken, disturbed, angry.

''I hate and despise him,'' she told herself desperately, then she flung herself on the bed and began to sob, muffling the sounds in her pillow.

It was dawn before she fell asleep. The cold light crept across the room and touched her tear-stained face on the pillow with a melancholy pallor. She closed her eyes against it, and at last sleep pulled her down into a healing darkness.

CHAPTER FOUR

A KNOCK on her door jolted her awake. She turned over reluctantly, wincing at the light, and raised herself on one elbow.

"Mmm?" Sleep muffled her voice, but apparently Adam heard her mumble enquiringly, because he came into the room, wearing a blue jeans suit and carrying a tray.

Kit peered out of sleep-bleared eyes. "W-what time is it?"

He placed the tray on her bedside table and surveyed her drily, hands on his hips.

"Ten o'clock of a bright summer morning, and you should be up and ready for some sightseeing," he told her unsympathetically. "I gather you didn't sleep too well."

Her tumbled bed was eloquent of a disturbed night. She sat up, yawning, pushing back the ruffled red-gold curls. "I'm always the same in a strange bed."

He looked amused. "Of course," he said smoothly. "I managed to persuade the kitchen to give me a tray."

The fragrance of coffee was filling the air, and Kit was suddenly hungry. She leaned over and poured herself a cup. Adam watched her, his grey eyes on the graceful curve of arm and breast, the cool white skin above her cotton nightdress. While she spread butter and cherry jam on a croissant, he walked to the window and stood staring out at the blue sky.

"Any ideas about where we should go today?" he asked.

"The usual places," she mumbled through a mouthful of buttery, melting croissant. "The Louvre, the Eiffel Tower, Notre Dame...I don't mind... anywhere in Paris will be great."

"Tomorrow I thought I'd hire a car and drive out to Versailles," he said.

"Fantastic! I'd love that!"

"I suppose you've seen it before?"

"I've been there, but it's so vast that one could never really get tired of it, or exhaust its possibilities..."

"Like a woman," he drawled. "All women have the capacity to be surprising just when you think you know them to the depths of their souls."

She concentrated on her coffee, her cheeks pink.

After a moment, Adam moved away from the window. "I'll leave you to get dressed. I'll give you fifteen minutes."

They made their first call at the Louvre. Slowly they moved through the galleries, gazing silently at the paintings, among a shuffling throng of other tourists. Children sat outside in the sunshine eating ice-cream, while souvenir sellers watched with lacklustre eyes as the tourists moved to and fro along the pavements. Kit's feet began to ache with the heat of city streets.

They talked about the paintings as they moved on to the Eiffel Tower. Adam was disposed to prefer High Renaissance art, but Kit had a powerful attachment to earlier, medieval work. "They're so mysterious and romantic yet so down to earth. Look at the faces, almost modern in the way they're presented, yet charged with a sort of mysticism you never find in later art."

Adam looked thoughtfully at her. "Mystic earthiness? A curious combination for you to like..."

"Do you want to go up the Tower?" Kit asked him, staring up at the rearing ironwork towering above them. "Or shall we have lunch?"

Adam grinned. "Hungry again already? No, we'll do the Tower first, then have lunch. I've booked a table for one o'clock and it's only just after twelve."

From the top of the Tower they looked out over a strange, grey Paris, the buildings a jumble of roofs, spires, towers patched in with the green of trees here and there. They picked out landmarks and looked out beyond the city to the distant countryside, followed the bending river as it flowed through the heart of the city, curving around the Ile de la Cité.

"I wonder what Paris looked like in the Middle Ages," Kit murmured aloud.

A short, stooping man in a crumpled suit spoke, surprising them. "I can tell you, *mademoiselle*. It was much smaller, of course, and contained within the old city walls, the remains of which you can trace even today. Paris remained largely a medieval walled city until the Revolution, when the expansion largely took place..." He talked quickly, in colloquial French which Kit only just managed to follow. "I am a lecturer in French history," he informed them. His picture of medieval Paris was concise and fascinating. He knew the names of every street and alley, even the names of shops and the whereabouts of hotels and wine shops.

Kit was given a vivid picture of Paris before the Revolution; she could imagine the narrow, dirty crowded streets infested with sullen humanity whose resentment towards their noble masters would soon spill over into the excesses of the Terror.

Later, as they left the Tower, Adam said with amusement, "How you manage to attract old men! First Count Theo, now that fellow... You have the strangest tastes."

"He was sweet," she defended. "He enjoyed telling us about Paris and I enjoyed hearing him..."

"You know who he was?" Adam asked drily. "Only one of the foremost French historians, Jules Presquieu!"

She was startled. "He said he was only a lecturer!"

"Modesty, no doubt," said Adam. "I recognised him because we once made a programme about the Revolution, and he was one of the men we interviewed. His books are best-sellers over here."

Kit glanced back up the Tower. "I wish I'd known!"

"It was because you didn't know that he was so unselfconscious," Adam told her. "Your pleasure in what he told you was reward enough for him, I suspect. Even great historians love to have a wide-eyed admiring audience, and you certainly provided him with that! You listened with bated breath. I doubt if his university students ever give him such rapt attention." He gave her a curiously veiled glance. "Count Theo hit the nail on the head. You're Desdemona, all right..."

She flushed. "You make me sound like an idiot!"

"I imagine there's an Othello buried in every man," Adam said drily. "What male could resist those big eyes, that admiring stare?"

They took their time over lunch, enjoying the superb food and wine. Kit carefully chose melon to start with, followed by coq au vin in a little earthenware casserole, with fresh strawberries and thick whipped cream to follow. Adam skipped the dessert and had Camembert. The restaurant was charming, decorated in Louis Quinze style, with silky brocade wallpaper and pale carpets which hushed every sound the waiters made around the tables.

After lunch they took a taxi to Montmartre. Artists crammed the narrow, hilly winding streets. Under leafy shades they had set up easels and were selling portraits to tourists prepared to sit for them. Kit at first refused to let Adam pay for a picture of herself, but he insisted, so she took a seat on a stool and a thin dark young man deftly sketched her with a pencil which moved confidently over the paper. From time to time he would pause, stare at her, then scratch away once more. Grave-eyed, she waited, while Adam leaned against a tree and watched.

At last the young man gestured finality, and she and Adam stared at the pencil sketch.

"Very good," Adam congratulated the artist. "You've caught her expression..."

Kit was surprised to see what the artist had made of her. She had been drawn in serious mood, her eyes fixed away in the distance, her profile fine and delicate.

"I look...like a boy," she said, half disliking it.

Adam accepted the sketch, rolled it up and put it under his arm. As they walked away he said quietly, "You look like a young saint," he said.

She was embarrassed by the comparison, and laughed.

Adam glanced at her sideways. "I would have expected you to be pleased with it—it's just what you were praising earlier, a mixture of mysticism and reality. Those curls of yours, your little neck and your high cheekbones...that boy caught a medieval look about you which I'd never noticed before, but which is definitely there once one looks for it."

"You must tell J.K.," she grinned. "He'll never believe you. He used to say I reminded him of a naughty schoolgirl."

"Everyone has different moods, all of which are true to one aspect of themselves. You can be mischievous—I've seen you like that, too. You can be sulky. Like most women, you have a hundred different facets..."

Kit flushed. "Thanks!"

"Why do you hate to hear yourself talked about? Most women love it. They're their own favourite subject."

"I'm not most women."

"True," he admitted. "I forgot. You're a mystery and an enigma..."

"Oh, shut up!" she said furiously.

He laughed. "Poor Katherine Mary! Are you at war with yourself? I can almost see your instincts struggling against that cold little brain of yours."

"What instincts?" she asked involuntarily, then wished she had not asked.

"You know very well what I mean."

"I don't," she denied.

"Well, if you must have it in simple language," he drawled, "you have the healthy sexual instincts of a young woman in her prime, but you for some reason feel compelled to repress them..."

"If you mean I didn't agree to jump into bed with you at a moment's notice, you're right," she said angrily. "That isn't repression, believe me. It's dislike of sex for its own sake. We're not in love. You've always been a total beast to me until the last few days. Suddenly, because we're in Paris alone, you seem to think I'm at your disposal whenever you feel like it. Well, you couldn't be more wrong. When I choose to respond it will be towards a man I love, not some comparative stranger."

"You responded right enough," Adam said tightly. He was suddenly taut, his skin pale with anger. "In the taxi coming back your response was pretty conclusive. I didn't pounce on a reluctant shrinking virgin, remember. It was a mutual explosion..."

"I was drunk," she said harshly.

"That's a damned lie!" He stopped, gripping her arm. "You'd had a few glasses of wine and one brandy, but you were by no means drunk. Neither was I. I was completely in control of myself."

"Let go of me. You're hurting!" she snapped.

He glared at her, his face dark with rage. "I'd like to hurt you. You make me furious. For days you've been flirting with me outrageously, but as soon as I make a move you slap me down like a wicked seducer in some Victorian melodrama. You know, there's a name for girls like you. You're a tease, and teases sometimes get more than they bargained for."

Kit tugged at her arm and he let go. She rubbed the red mark he had made, her face resentful. "You're a brute! Look at that...there'll be a bruise there tomorrow."

"Perhaps it'll teach you a lesson," he snapped. "If you play with dynamite it often explodes."

She walked on and he caught up with her. They walked in total silence for a while until their hotel came into view, then Adam said tightly, "Perhaps you would like to go back to England tomorrow instead of visiting Versailles?"

"That's your decision," she said coldly. "You're in charge of this trip, not me..."

He made an irritated movement, but said nothing for a while. As they were in the little green lift he said coolly, "We might as well stay until Monday, I suppose."

"As you wish," she said indifferently.

They separated at their rooms. Kit sank down on her bed and surveyed the wreckage of the day with miserable eyes. Why did they keep quarrelling? Why was Adam such a pig? She ran her fingers through her short curls. She would not let him ruin her lovely weekend in Paris. Tomorrow she would feast her eyes on the splendours of Versailles and ignore him.

Defiantly she glanced at her watch. It was five o'clock. Would the shops still be open? She left her room again, caught the lift down and went out in search of a new dress, something to make Adam realise that she was a sophisticated young woman, not a frightened child.

She found a small boutique in a back street. The proprietress was just about to close, but agreed to find her something suitable.

"Something startling," Kit expounded.

The small, thin dark woman eyed her knowingly. "For a man?" she asked softly.

Kit flushed. Then she shrugged. "I want to look different," she said haltingly. "I want to..." She paused, searching for the right words.

"To hit him between the eyes?" said the woman in excellent English.

Kit laughed, very pink. "Something like that."

"I understand. We will do what we can. With your colouring it will not be easy, but I think I may have something..."

When she returned she carried a dress over her arm. The material was silkily clinging, the colour a lustrous sea green. The Frenchwoman helped Kit into it, then stood back with a sigh of satisfaction. "That is it," she said with a nod.

Kit surveyed herself in the mirror with mounting excitement. It certainly was it, she agreed. The dress was cut expertly to mould her body where it touched, from breasts to thigh. The neckline was frankly revealing, plunging in a deep V to follow the line of the breasts, making her look even more slender at the waist but giving a new sexiness to her body. It fell to her feet, swishing silkily as she moved. Simple, eye-catching and provocative, it was just what she had envisaged when she came in here.

She shivered. "It's fantastic," she agreed. "But...I feel half naked..."

The Frenchwoman laughed. "You are too modest. Believe me, it will have the effect you desire. If not, return it. I will give you back your money—I guarantee it."

Kit smiled. "Oh, I believe you. I only wonder if I have the nerve to wear it!"

"There are times in life when one must be bold," said the other woman. "Seize life, *chérie*. Do not let it escape you."

Kit sighed. "You're right, of course." She thought of Adam's face when he saw it. Her pride demanded that she force him to...to what? she asked herself, then shied away from answering the question.

She smiled at the woman. "How much?"

The sum made her gasp, and the Frenchwoman shrugged. "For a dress like this one must pay!"

Kit found her travellers cheques, counted them and groaned to herself, but paid with a smile. The other woman had been very sympathetic and helpful, after all.

Back in her hotel room she laid the dress out on the bed and gazed at it lovingly. She would wear it for dinner tonight. They were dining at the hotel. She went into the bathroom to begin her preparations, first careful to lock her door. Adam had a habit of bursting into her room, and she did not want him to see her dress until she was ready.

She had agreed to meet him in the Royal Bar downstairs at seven o'clock for a pre-dinner drink. She had only just enough time now to shower, put on her make-up and do her hair.

She was relieved not to meet him as she made her way to the lift. She wanted to make a grand entrance, to watch his face as he first saw her. Her pulses were hammering violently as she emerged on the ground floor and swept towards the swing doors which led to the Royal Bar.

Without looking round, she sensed the impression she was making on those people in the foyer who looked round to stare at her. She heard conversations still and then begin again in whispered comment.

A pageboy leapt to one side, eyeing her admiringly, and Kit smiled at him, grateful for this first reaction. She had never in her life worn such an expensive dress, or felt so aware of herself. She most usually wore jeans or skirts and jumpers. Tonight she felt a new person, a stranger, alluringly gowned and conscious of her own looks.

The Royal Bar was a semi-circle of chairs arranged around a long curved bar. The carpets were royal blue. Brocade curtains hung at the tall windows. The deep armchairs were of cream leather studded with brass. In groups of two or three they stood around low tables on which were tiny blue pots of flowers.

There were a number of people in the room already, and Kit paused to glance around. She saw Adam before he saw her. He was in evening clothes, looking even more elegantly attractive than usual, his formidable strength smoothed into urbanity by the dark cloth. He was sitting at a table by a window, turned sideways to her, and facing him was a very beautiful woman in a short cream silk dress.

Kit watched them, wondering if Adam was with a friend, or had just made this woman's acquaintance. While she watched, Adam laughed easily, and the other woman laid a slender white hand on his knee briefly, a familiar gesture which made Kit stiffen. A bitter pang shot through her. She bit her lip, then released it and moved forward.

Adam turned his head casually as she joined them, then did a double-take, eyeing her almost with disbelief, his grey eyes sliding from the alluring curve of her bodice to the sleekness of the clinging lower folds. She saw his eyes narrow, the swift upward flick of his lids towards her face.

He stood up and drew back the third chair. "What will you have to drink?" he asked.

"A Martini, thank you," she said, sinking into the leather armchair with a silken swish.

He introduced his companion casually. "Elena, this is Kit Ashley. Kit, an old friend of mine—Elena Demetriou. Elena is the widow of Nick Demetriou, one of the best TV reporters Greece has produced."

Elena offered Kit a faint smile of appraisal. She was a dark woman, with smooth olive skin and black eyes, her mouth wide and passionate, her expression assertively assured.

"I remember seeing your husband reporting on the political changes in Greece just before his death," Kit said. "I was very sorry to hear about that. He was a fine man."

Elena inclined her head with dignity. "Nick was too brave. The brave pay dearly for their courage. I always knew he would die violently."

"A stray bullet in an African guerilla camp or death in a car crash, no one is quite sure how it happened," Adam told Kit. "Nick was reported killed in Africa, but the true story never emerged. There are several versions. You can believe which you choose."

"I do not care how it happened," Elena said. "That it did happen was enough for me." She shrugged her slender shoulders. "We had five good years, and I am grateful for that."

"Have you any children?" Kit asked her.

Elena glanced at her coldly. "No." The monosyllable was glacial. Kit flushed, regretting the question.

Adam said, "Elena, another Campari for you?"

She smiled at him with intimate warmth. "Darling, you mustn't encourage me to drink! I'm dining with a very important, very boring French minister. I want him to get drunk and tell me everything, but I must keep a cool head tonight."

"Lucky minister," Adam drawled. "What about a drink after you get rid of him?"

Elena wrinkled her nose. "Who knows? It depends how things go. I'll come in here if I'm free at about ten—but don't count on it!" She glanced at the clock above the door. "He will be here in a moment. I do not want to be seen with you, *chéri*, you are far too handsome. It will make him jealous, and I need to get him into a good mood. I must go." She stood up, bent gracefully and kissed Adam with frank sensuality on the mouth, her fingers touching his cheek. "Mmm, how I wish you were an important politician, *chéri*! Such an interview I could enjoy!"

"What a charming idea," Adam drawled.

Elena laughed. "What do you English call it ... a pipe dream? A fantasy? We all have them, no?" She gave Kit a brief, cool nod and moved away with easy, graceful steps, like a ballet dancer, her slender legs very elegant.

Kit leaned back, bitterly aware that Elena's presence had ruined her great entrance. The other woman had been truly sophisticated, a woman of the world, sensual, experienced, intelligent, the sort of woman Adam no doubt customarily took out. Kit's own masquerade had been revealed for what it was—a mere mimicry of the thing.

Adam sipped his drink, looking at her over the rim of his glass with expressionless eyes.

"That dress has Paris stamped all over it," he drawled. "When did you get that?"

"Tonight," she admitted.

His lip curled sardonically. "What was it supposed to do? Bring me crashing to the floor? Is that what you want, Kit? To have your man on his knees at your feet while like a goddess you gaze down at him from your untouched heights?"

"Could I have another Martini?" she asked, ignoring his remarks.

He snapped his fingers and a waiter appeared to take the order. Adam finished his own drink hastily and received another, while Kit played with her glass, unable to meet his eyes. She felt foolish. Her plan had been childishly blatant. Adam had seen through it at once.

They drank their drinks in silence, then Adam stood up. "Shall we have dinner now?"

She nodded. They left the bar and went through into the long dining-room. Their table was ready for them, decorated with one long-stemmed white rose in a thin green vase. The waiter hovered expectantly. They ordered quite quickly, and were soon eating the *pâté de la maison* with triangles of crisp, hot toast

which was served wrapped in a damask napkin. The
pâté was country-made, spiced with herbs and nutty
with flavour.

Adam said so little that Kit began to feel thoroughly ill at ease. Her plan had backfired on her. She
had annoyed him. She herself was not quite sure what
she had hoped to achieve, except that she had ob-
scurely felt she wanted to make him look at her in a
way he never had before. Why she wanted this she did
not know. It had been a confused desire buried deep
within her subconscious.

Why? she asked herself desperately. Why did I want
to get that look from him? Is he right? Did I want him
on his knees? She pushed aside her plate and bit her
lip. Honesty compelled her to admit to herself that she
wanted Adam to look at her as he had looked at
Elena—with the frank admiration of a male for a desirable female. Until now he had treated her teasingly, with the control of a much older man towards a
young girl, and Kit wanted something else from him.
She drew back instinctively from her own thoughts.
Her mind was full of hidden abysses, she told herself
in shock.

They finished their meal still in the same uneasy silence. While they drank their coffee Adam gazed
moodily across the restaurant to where Elena sat with
her middle-aged French politician, flirting discreetly
with him.

Kit wished herself back in England. Things were not
going well here.

"There's dancing in the cabaret room," Adam told
her. "Do you want to dance? It's too early to turn
in . . ."

She agreed politely, and they moved through into the much smaller inner room, where tables were set up around a tiny dance floor. A cabaret took place at eleven, but at the moment a few couples were dancing to a small band.

Adam led Kit on to the floor. His arm gripped her casually around the waist and they began to move to the rhythmic beat of the music. The band were playing a waltz. With amusement Kit saw that they were an English band, and that several of the acts scheduled for the cabaret, according to a poster beside the band dais, were also English.

Adam's hand moved convulsively, pulling her closer. She felt the muscled hardness of his chest against her, the movement of his thighs as they turned and glided, and her heart began to beat faster. Her mouth was suddenly dry with inexplicable excitement.

Suddenly Adam halted and his hand dropped away from her. Kit looked up, startled, her eyes wide.

He was frowning, his skin pale, his mouth taut. "Let's sit down," he said thickly.

They sat at a table a little apart from the others. Kit saw a waiter hurry forward to take their order. Adam ordered a whisky for himself, a gin and orange for her. He leaned back, scowling, his eyebrows a black bar across his face. Kit was puzzled and alarmed by his expression. He glanced at her as he lifted his glass to his mouth.

Then he said, deeply, "This wasn't a good idea."

She frowned. "What wasn't?"

"Dancing," Adam said.

"I'm sorry. I know I don't dance very well," she said, with a humiliated blink. "Waltzing isn't done much in London clubs. We tend to do more modern dances."

He brushed her words away with irritation. "I didn't mean that. You know damned well what I mean..."

"I don't," she said blankly.

His grey eyes met her look with a steely impatience. "Having you in my arms and pretending to be civilised and polite is more than flesh and blood can stand," he snapped. "That dress is a deliberate come-on...you know damned well you only wore it to make me want to take it off...and if it pleases you, then O.K., its had the effect you wanted! It sent my temperature through the roof. But don't deliberately invite me, then expect me to act like a little wooden gentleman, because I don't play that sort of game."

Her pulses began to race violently. She lowered her gaze, then looked at him through her lashes. "I thought you didn't like my dress?"

He swore under his breath. "My God, you ask for trouble! What sort of girl are you? I think we'd better leave before I make a public spectacle of myself."

"I'm not tired," she said softly.

Adam's look made her tingle with excitement. "You're pushing me too far, Kit," he ground out thickly.

She sighed. "Can't we dance again?"

Adam bit his lower lip. "Well, I've warned you," he said at last.

They stood up and walked back on to the floor. Adam pulled her close, his hand possessively hard against her back, and Kit sank against him with a little sigh of pleasure. As they began to dance, Adam said in her ear, "You intoxicate me...that look of surrender drives me mad...I knew that was how you could look..."

She whispered, "I thought I was a frozen spinster? Have you changed your mind?"

Deeply he said, "I think you've changed yours..."

Kit stiffened. "Not in the way you mean. I'm not built for promiscuity, Adam. Don't misunderstand..."

He drew back and looked sharply at her. "Now what are you up to? This isn't another change of mood, is it? Are you determined to drive me berserk?"

"I don't go to bed with everyone I dance with," she retorted.

"I should hope not," he said coldly.

The music came to an end. They stood looking at each other, close together but not touching. Kit's eyes were wide, fringed with dark lashes, her pink mouth moistly parted on a sigh.

"Must we quarrel all the time?"

"Don't give me that appealing little-girl look," he growled. "It doesn't go with the dress."

His glance hardened on her face for a moment, as if he debated something within himself, then he glanced at his watch.

"I'm afraid you must excuse me now. I've got a date, remember?" His dark face was mocking. "With Elena..."

He walked her out of the bar, his hand just below her elbow. More than distance lay between them. Kit

felt icy cold with pain and a jealousy new to her.
Adam saw her into the lift, gave her a last nod and
walked away.

He was going to Elena, who was experienced and
subtle, who knew what she wanted and was prepared
to reach out for it. Elena would not be a party to
scruples about love. She would take pleasure where she
found it and ask no questions, make no further demands.

Kit found herself in her own room without realising how she got there. The dim reflection of herself in
the mirror mocked her cruelly. The alluring dress
looked hateful to her now. She stripped it off hurriedly, flung it on the floor and went into the bathroom. Cold water stung her awake, erased the
lingering hungriness Adam had aroused in her body.

She slid into bed and found a book in her bedside
cabinet. She read a few dull pages, rubbed her eyes
childishly, then glanced at her new dress. It lay in a
silken, gleaming heap. She sighed, got out of bed and
shook it out, hung it up carefully. It was too expensive for such cavalier treatment. She grimaced. Edward would love it and be slightly shocked by it. She
faced herself once more in the mirror. Her face was
flushed, washed clean of all make-up, and she looked
very young. Anyway, she told her reflection, I hate
Adam. I hate him! If Elena and her kind are what he
wants, let him have them! I was perfectly happy not so
long ago. I can be so again. This is just a temporary
madness. It's the effect of Paris in June. I'll get over
it. I'm not in love, after all. Her reflection gazed back
at her mockingly. Aren't you? her eyes asked.

She spoke aloud, defiantly. "No, I'm not...not with him! And I hate him..."

Then she tumbled into bed once more and put out the light. In the darkness she heard the distant roar of Paris traffic, reminiscent of the far-off whisper of the sea, a sound which, city-bred, she found soothing as only city dwellers can. She lay wide-eyed in the dark room thinking of Adam, remembering with pulsing excitement what he had said. She had certainly aroused him as planned, but she had not been prepared for the violence of his reactions, or indeed for the sensual hunger he might arouse in herself.

She groaned, turning over to bury her face in the pillow. Just the image of his dark face, the desire openly reflected in his grey eyes, was sufficient to make her shake with passionate response. She did not know how to cope with it. Like a child playing with fire, she had set light to herself as well as Adam, and now she did not know how to deal with the situation she had deliberately created.

CHAPTER FIVE

SURPRISINGLY, she had slept quite well, emotionally exhausted by what had happened the evening before, and she was up and dressed by eight o'clock.

She was wearing her cream pleated skirt and a tight-fitting cream sweater. She threaded a wide black velvet bandeau through her curls and slipped into flat black shoes, then went down to the dining-room.

Adam was already at the table, studying a map of Paris and its suburbs. He glanced up as she joined him, his expression cool.

"Good morning."

Kit sat down and reached for the coffee pot. "Did you sleep well?" she asked him with the polite interest of a stranger.

"Yes, thank you. Did you?" He sipped his own coffee, watching as she spread butter on a croissant.

"Very," she said, half defiantly.

Their eyes met briefly. "We'll leave as soon as you've finished breakfast," he said. "The car is already outside in the hotel car park. It was delivered at seven-thirty, they tell me."

She bit into her croissant. It was warm and flaky, utterly delicious. Taking a sip of coffee, she glanced at Adam through her lashes. He was looking coldly imperturbable.

"Adam," she began hesitantly, "I ... I'm sorry about last night ... I realise I behaved in a very silly fashion. We're here on a job, not to play games ..."

He regarded her enigmatically. "Is that what you were doing? Playing games? A dangerous game to play, Kit."

She shrugged. "Yes, I'm sorry."

He leaned back in his chair. "You've always been a spoilt little madam. Your uncle gave you too much. He wanted to make up to you for losing your parents, I suppose, but he forgot that you can go too far with that sort of spoiling."

Stung, she retorted, "That isn't true, J.K. never spoilt me!"

"You had a sports car for your eighteenth birthday, remember? Another dangerous toy for a girl to play with! And J.K. always gave you anything you asked for, even a job in the studios which he knew very well would put people's backs up."

"I've worked hard at my job," she said, bitterly hurt.

Adam inclined his head. "I'm aware of that. I would never have put up with anything less from you than from any other member of the team. I've seen to it that you pulled your weight. I won't deny I was impressed by the work you've done. But underneath all that, you're still the little rich girl who's been spoon-fed by a doting bachelor uncle all her life. What you're looking for in a man isn't the equal give and take of a marriage partnership. You want the doting adoration J.K. has always given you."

"No!" Kit pushed away her plate and stood up. Adam followed her into the hotel foyer, caught her arm and guided her through a side door to the car park.

Quietly, he murmured, "Think about what I've said. You'll find it's true."

She slid into the passenger seat of the car he had hired. As he climbed in beside her she said angrily, "You're just making these accusations because I wasn't prepared to play the sort of game you prefer. I'm old-fashioned about love. Men have fed me clever lines before now...told me I was out of date or hinted that I was repressed...all girls get that sort of approach. It doesn't work, Adam. I know what I want, believe me."

He drove coolly out of the car park and turned into the flow of Paris traffic. "And what do you want?" he asked her casually.

"Out-of-date, old-fashioned love," she said defiantly. "The sort in books. It exists. I have friends who found it. It isn't based on sex alone, it's based on mutual feelings of trust and kindness, caring and sharing. It lasts to eternity because it's solid and real."

"I shall never get married," Adam said calmly. "I don't believe in it. I saw my parents tearing each other apart for years before my mother finally committed suicide..."

Kit stared at him, shocked and compassionate. "Oh, how terrible for you...how old were you?"

"When she killed herself? Fifteen."

Kit closed her eyes briefly. "Poor Adam! The very worst time. Just when you were at your most vulnerable, most sensitive..."

Adam spoke harshly, "I got over it. She didn't. Marriage killed her. My father wouldn't divorce her, and she couldn't leave him for fear of losing me. He would never have let her take me with her.''

"But she left you in the end," Kit said gently.

"He had already separated us by sending me to school two hundred miles away." Adam's face was grim. "God knows what she suffered at his hands, alone in that house.''

"What about your father? How did he take it?''

"He married again," Adam said savagely. "An attractive woman he'd been seeing long before my mother died. I never lived with him again. I went up to university at eighteen, and from then on I avoided him. I haven't seen him for ten years.''

"I can see why you feel as you do," Kit said gently. "But, Adam, because one marriage ends badly it doesn't mean they all do. Your parents didn't love each other, that's all.''

"They did once," Adam said. "My mother told me so. But it died and they lived in permanent warfare for years. It poisoned their whole lives. Rather than finish a relationship like that, I would avoid marriage altogether. You have a romantic view of it. Love doesn't live eternally, and when it dies you're left tied to each other like two savage animals. You savage each other and destroy everything around you.''

"Yet you said your friend Elena was happy with her husband, Nick.''

"They were happy, yes, but it was already wearing thin. Nick had other women, and Elena knew about it. She still loved him, but she wasn't faithful either. How long would their marriage have survived the strain of infidelity, do you think?''

Kit glanced at him. What had happened between him and Elena last night? she wondered bitterly. It was none of her business what he did in his private life, of course. But she could not help imagining all sorts of things, picturing Adam with Elena in his arms, that passionate hunger in his dark face as he kissed her mouth and throat, exploring the supple elegance of her body at will without fearing rejection. They were both experienced adults. Kit bit her lip jealously. Had he slept with Elena last night? She longed to ask him, yet dared not, partly for fear of what the question would reveal of herself and partly because she just did not want to know for certain. To know that he had made love to Elena would be to turn the thorn of jealousy into her heart and twist it.

Adam glanced at her sideways, a smile of mockery on his lean features.

"You have a very expressive face," he told her suddenly. "I can read your every thought. And the answer to your unasked question is no, I did not make love to Elena last night."

Colour flooded into her face. "I . . . I wasn't thinking anything of the kind," she lied.

He laughed. "Perhaps I leapt to conclusions, but I doubt it. We were talking of Elena and you gave me some very funny looks."

"Did I?" She tried to look casual. "Well, why didn't you?"

"Why not?" Adam raised a dark eyebrow. "Perhaps because Elena was otherwise occupied with her French politician."

Kit stared at him. "Otherwise you would have done, I suppose?"

"She's a very sexy lady," he agreed cheerfully. "In many ways we see things from the same point of view. We're old friends."

"Friends!" She exclaimed bitterly. "Is that what you call friendship?"

"I told you I don't believe in platonic friendship, remember?" He looked amused.

"You don't believe in anything much at all, do you? You don't believe in love or friendship... was Elena your mistress while her husband was alive? Or didn't you get... friendly... then?"

"I'm not in the habit of seducing my friends' wives, no," he said, suddenly angry. "And I do believe in love. It's marriage I don't believe in ..."

"Love? You call your sexual acrobatics love?" Kit was white with anger. "You don't know the meaning of the word!"

"You're angry with me for shattering your romantic dream of love and happy every after," Adam said calmly. "I'm sorry if I've disillusioned you, but it had to happen some day. You can't go around with stars in your eyes for the rest of your life."

"You're wrong," Kit said icily. "I can, and I intend to do so. I'll find my romantic dream one day. I'm sorry for you, Adam. You've had a rotten experience, but you've let it poison your whole attitude to life. You're not destroying my dreams, though. My parents loved each other until the day they died, and ours was a perfectly happy home. I mean to make sure my own marriage is like that."

"Marriage to whom? The smooth, dull Edward?" Adam was at his most sarcastic.

"No, Edward isn't the man," she admitted. "But I'll find him one day, I know I will."

The car leapt forward. Adam stared straight ahead, his hands gripping the wheel, doing eighty miles an hour along the straight French road. Kit grew alarmed. The expression on his face made her nervous. He looked grimly angry.

"You're going too fast," she said.

He glanced at her, then relaxed and the needle dropped slowly to sixty again. "I'm sorry. Did I frighten you?"

"Yes," she admitted frankly. "Why did you suddenly drive so fast?"

He shrugged. "Perhaps your woolly-minded romanticism suddenly infuriated me."

"You mean you resent my refusal to see the world through your black-tinted glasses?"

Adam said coolly, "I mean I fancy you like hell, and I was facing the fact that I was never going to get what I want unless I paid a price I refuse to pay."

Kit swallowed, feeling suddenly weak-kneed. "I see," she whispered tremulously.

There was a pause while Adam drove and she leaned back, trying desperately to sort out her tangled thoughts. Then she said huskily, "Are you hinting that . . . you love me . . . in your own way, Adam?"

"I would rather not use that word," he said brusquely. "I've already put it as plainly as I can. I want to make love to you. I find you beautiful and desirable and I find it hard to keep my hands off you. When you ask if I love you, I find the question unanswerable because we aren't using the same terms of reference, I suspect."

"You mean you would like to sleep with me?" she asked in a very quiet little voice.

"Just that," Adam said crisply.

"Just as you enjoy sleeping with other women? With Elena, for instance, or any one of the models you go around with in London?"

Adam stared straight. "I refuse to make comparisons."

"But that is what you mean?"

"Don't keep probing, for God's sake," he said in infuriated tones. "I've told you how I feel. I know how you feel. We've been totally frank with each other and we both know how the matter stands. What else is there to say?"

Huskily, Kit said, "There is one thing I must say, Adam. I find it insulting, not flattering, that you should regard me as another of your playmates, to be taken to bed when you're in the mood and dropped when you're after someone new. There's a very ugly word for you. I won't use it, but I must ask you never to speak to me on the subject again. I never want to hear another word about it." She swallowed bitterly. "You make me sick . . ."

Adam grimaced wryly. "Direct, aren't you? All right, I'll promise never to raise the matter again. From now on, we're just colleagues. It will be a purely working arrangement."

"That's fine by me," Kit said acidly.

The green shade of Fontainebleau came into sight, and by mutual consent they dropped the subject.

THE MAGNIFICENCE of Versailles was already a fading memory as they flew back to England on a grey

Monday morning. They landed at midday and drove back to London through spears of fine rain. The countryside looked green and tranquil. The roads were by contrast choked with traffic.

Adam dropped her at her flat. "I'll get in touch with Count Theo's secretary today and get her to give me the address of his farmer friend," he said casually.

"Shall I report to J.K.?" Kit asked, leaning down to look at him in his car.

Adam shrugged. "As you like. We have little to report, have we?"

"You know how he hates to get big expenses sheets without explanation," she pointed out. "It's always best to warn him in advance when you've spent a lot on expenses."

"Especially when you have little to show for it?" Adam asked drily.

She shrugged again. "We didn't achieve much, did we?"

"Oh, I don't know," Adam said pointedly. "I wouldn't say that."

She withdrew her head in a hurry. "Well, good-bye," she called, marching in to the house.

It was comforting to be back in her own flat again, surrounded by reassurances of home, but she was restless, prowling around without knowing quite what she was doing, picking up an ornament here, a book there, staring unseeingly out of the window.

She was depressed, she admitted to herself. It seemed a million years since she left this flat to fly to Paris with Adam, and so much had happened in the interval. She was reluctant to examine exactly what had happened. The thought of Adam pressed like a thorn into her consciousness. She winced away from memories of him, yet could not refrain from constantly permitting her thoughts to wander in his direction.

Did she love him? she asked herself brutally, but at once withdrew the question in alarm. Love was a gentle emotion. What she felt towards Adam was too violent, too contradictory to be love. Sometimes she felt she hated him. Sometimes she felt a warm confusion as she remembered the touch of his mouth, the intimate glance of his eyes. Her thoughts swung constantly. The only thing she was certain of was that she could not love him. It would be disastrous for any woman to fall in love with a man so possessed by the determination never to give himself. Any woman who was fool enough to let herself love him would go hungry all her life, her love unsatisfied, her caring unwanted.

The telephone rang, and she started. J.K., she thought guiltily, no doubt wanting to know why she had not immediately rung him on her return.

She picked up the receiver. "Hello?"

"I've been on to this chap Loxford," Adam said. "At least, I spoke to the manager of his farm. Loxford isn't there. He's in Scotland, fishing."

She groaned. "Oh, no! Well, that's that."

"I'm taking the night train," said Adam.

"Adam! You're becoming obsessed!"

"I don't give up easily," Adam retorted. "I want to know about Jan Watowski. I mean to find out everything I can, and there's not that much time. The programme has to be in the can before the autumn viewing starts."

She sighed. "Well, have a nice time in Scotland."

"We will," he said coolly. "Don't unpack. The train leaves at midnight."

"Midnight?" she shrieked. "Adam, I can't! I'm exhausted by the Paris trip. You don't need me."

"Oh, but I do," he said.

There was a little silence, then Kit murmured faintly, "Couldn't it wait until this man Loxford gets back?"

"No, I can't afford to lose a day. Unless I turn up a cracking good story, J.K. will insist that I use the Landell version of his life, and all my instincts tell me that there's a buried truth somewhere that ought to be brought out. I'd swear Landell doesn't have the real story of Watowski."

She sighed. "Oh, very well."

"I'll pick you up in a taxi," Adam said. "Be ready at eleven-fifteen."

"I'm never going to sleep on a train," she complained.

"You will," Adam said easily. "It is surprising."

"Couldn't we drive up there?"

"My God, girl, do you know how far it is to the Highlands of Scotland from London? I'd be dead on my feet if I drove all that way!"

"Oh, very well," she muttered. "I'll be ready."

"Have you rung J.K. yet?"

"No," she admitted. "I'll do that now."

"Fine," said Adam, and rang off without saying goodbye. Kit glared at the receiver, replacing it with a bang.

J.K. was amused by her version, discreetly edited, of the Paris trip. He queried the necessity for a trip to Scotland, but sighed.

"I suppose I'd better not argue with Adam over it. Adam can be so damned touchy. All the best producers are, unfortunately—egotists to the last man. Only their own opinion matters, and they won't have any interference in their work. Adam has resigned twice over some petty argument, but I can't afford to lose him. I know of at least two companies who would be delighted to buy him from us."

"I can't think why," said Kit bitterly.

J.K. laughed. "Still at daggers drawn, darling? Never mind. For my sake, be nice to Adam. Keep him happy."

"You don't know what you're asking," she groaned.

J.K. chuckled. "Don't I? I assure you I know he's an overbearing, arrogant fellow, but he's a brilliant man at his job. I have a great respect for his work. So be nice to him, Kit."

"I'll refrain from beating his head in with a blunt instrument," she said savagely. "That will be the best I can do." She groaned again. "Do you realise I have to catch a train at midnight to please him? Midnight, I ask you! I'll be dead on my feet tomorrow. Working with Adam Rothbury is like being part of Attila the Hun's army. One is constantly on the march, constantly lashed by his wicked tongue! The man's inhuman."

"Bear up, darling," J.K. said with a smile in his voice. "I'm sure it will be a great programme."

"Oh, that's all you care about!"

"No," he denied. "I care about you, and I hope you do manage to sleep on the train. Take care of yourself, Kit."

When she had hung up she paced around the room, then finished unpacking her case and repacked it with warmer, more practical clothes. Scotland was a different proposition from Paris. She packed jeans, sweaters, sensible brogue shoes. No doubt Adam would have her tramping across muddy fields to sit on cold river banks while he talked to this Loxford man!

She hesitated over her boutique model dress, then with a shrug hung it in the wardrobe. She would not need that, she told herself. There would be no occasion to wear it, and even if there was, she would not wish to attract Adam's interest ever again. She stared at it, hanging there, gleaming and silky, then with a flush of self-contempt took it down again and hurriedly packed it.

Who knew what might happen? she asked herself. Life was quite incalculable.

Adam picked her up as arranged, then drove to the station, paid off the taxi and hurried her through the echoing station hall towards their platform. Even at this late hour the place was thronged with travellers, and the tannoy system blared incomprehensibly from time to time, slurring the names of stations so that it was impossible to guess what was being said.

Adam had reserved a first-class compartment and two sleeping berths. They turned in almost at once, to Kit's relief, and although she lay sleepless for a long time she finally fell asleep and woke when the sleeping-car attendant brought her a cup of tea.

They ate breakfast together, looking out at the passing landscape with the ideal tranquillity of those who have nothing to do but enjoy themselves.

The coffee was excellent, the breakfast over adequate. Kit ate bacon and egg in a euphoric mood, delighted by the sunshine, the scenery and her own feeling of well being.

She was not familiar with Scotland, having rarely travelled there. The beauty of the countryside dazed her. Rolling heather moors, grey rock, green valleys and grey lochs succeeded one another time and again in a changing yet uniform pattern. There was a rugged grandeur about the landscape that was impressive.

"So you slept after all?" Adam asked her.

"Surprisingly well," she agreed.

"It's rather like being on a boat. The rocking motion can be very soothing," he nodded.

"I suppose so," she shrugged.

"I've been reading Watowski's poems again. I'm increasingly struck by the change in the later ones, and by odd gaps. There's that sonnet sequence, for instance. I could swear that something is missing from it. There are references to other sonnets which aren't in the sequence and printed nowhere in the book."

"Perhaps he didn't like them and threw them away? Poets do revise a lot."

"That's possible," Adam admitted.

They left the train sometime later, and took a slow local train to the little station of Lachnakyle. The train stopped at every station en route and took what seemed years to Kit, but at last they staggered out on to a clean-swept platform in the brisk morning air. The train reluctantly pulled out again leaving them with their cases around them.

A small man in a peaked cap and fisherman's waders peered at them from a cubbyhole.

"Was you for the fishing?" he asked doubtfully, eyeing their luggage and taking in the absence of fishing tackle. "There is only the Fisherman's rest to be staying at, and I do not say Tommy Mac has any rooms to spare just at the present. There's a party of English up there, do you see?"

"We are only here for a short time," Adam said. "We've come to see someone who's staying at the Fisherman's Rest."

The little man pushed back his cap and scratched his head. "Now would that be Sir Andrew, I wonder? Or Colonel Moran, perhaps? Or it might be Mr. Loxford, of course..."

Adam grinned. "Mr. Loxford it is," he said, amused by the man's deep interest.

"Oh, that would be it," the man nodded. "Yes, indeed. Mr. Loxford is up here. He is always here every year, forby he was serving with Tommy Mac in the war, d'ye see, and fast friends they wass and still are indeed. But the fishing has not been good this morning, I am sorry to say."

"Too much sun," agreed Adam, looking up at the bright sky.

"Aye, thatt is so," the little man nodded. "Now yesterday it wass very good fishing."

"Rained, did it?" Adam asked courteously.

"Spitted down all day, it did," the man said with pleasure. "Not heavy, mind, but a good spit, spit all day long, and the skies as dull as pea soup. The fish wass rising beautiful."

A car drew up outside the little station with a screech of tyres, and a door banged. Footsteps sounded on the ancient boards of the platform, then a tall young man in a very ancient green sweater and old corduroy trousers hurried round the corner. He stopped when he saw them, his glance taking in Kit with a widening of the eyes.

"Hello! Are you Mr. Rothbury?" he asked Adam.

Adam smiled. "Yes. You can't be Mr. Loxford?"

"Thiss is Sir Andrew," intervened the small man with a shocked expression.

"Andrew Dudley," the young man added with a grin, shaking Adam's hand. "Loxford asked me to pick you up as I had to pass the station on my way back from the village." He looked again at Kit.

Adam introduced her and the young man shook hands with her appreciatively. "I say, you'll be a welcome addition to the party. I hope you're staying for a while? Fishing is great sport, but it can be boring in the intervals. Today is a complete write-off, for instance. No chance of a bite while the sun shines like this. All we do is play cards and argue."

Kit laughed. "It sounds very peaceful."

"Oh, it's all right," he nodded. "I've been here for a week, though, and my desire for peace is pretty well assuaged, I think. I'm beginning to long for some company more my own age." He gave her a confiding grin. "The other members of our party are all my father's generation. He used to come every year. They're all ex-pilots, you know. It was a sort of get-together they dreamed up during the war. They kept it up, too. After Dad died they invited me along in his place. I enjoy the fishing, and this place is delightful, but I sometimes feel a bit of an odd-man-out."

Adam asked brusquely. "Did they all serve in the same squadron, by any chance?"

"Yes, they did," Sir Andrew agreed. He looked curiously at Adam. "I gathered from George that that was why you wanted to see him. Something about that Polish chap? A lot of Poles flew in the Royal Air Force, didn't they?"

Adam nodded. Kit got the impression that he had not taken to Sir Andrew. An air of hostility emanated from him beneath his courtesy.

Sir Andrew picked up Kit's case and moved towards the exit. Adam followed with his own luggage. Outside the station stood a sleek little sports car. Sir Andrew stowed the luggage in the boot, helped Kit into the passenger seat and deprecatingly indicated that Adam would have to perch on the back. "Really only built for two," he explained, letting out the engine with a deafening roar.

The little man in the peaked cap waved to them cheerfully, and Sir Andrew and Kit waved back. Adam grimly stared ahead.

The road was pretty bumpy, almost a farm track, and led only to a small inn beside a tree-fringed river. The whitewashed walls bulged under their thatched roof. The windows winked back at the sun, their lintels massive and their sills very narrow. There was a simple, rugged strength about the rambling building. It was built in an L-shape, with outhouses forming the cross-piece of the L. A horse grazed in a rough paddock beside the gate. Two estate cars were parked on gravel to one side.

"I expect everyone is in the bar," said Sir Andrew. "Just coming up to lunchtime. That's where we'll find them, drowning their sorrows."

The bar was a small, square room facing the river. A handful of men lounged in armchairs, glasses in their hands. They rose in confusion as Kit entered.

"Good God," muttered a stoutly choleric-looking man. "A woman!"

Adam glanced at her with amusement, then looked round the semi-circle of curious faces. A very thin, tall man in a thick white fisherman's jersey and old cord trousers came forward, his hand extended.

"You must be Rothbury. I'm Loxford—George."

"I'm Adam," came the reply. "This is my assistant, Kit."

George Loxford shook Kit's hand dubiously. "I'm afraid we were not expecting a young lady," he said. "The truth is, there's going to be a bit of an accommodation problem. We can fit another chap in quite easily. We intended you to share Andy's room, Adam, but there isn't another room available."

"No problem," said Sir Andrew hastily. "Tell you what! I'll pitch a tent in the paddock. Adam and I could share that, then Kit can have my room. I enjoy camping, especially in fine weather like this..."

"I couldn't let you do that," Kit protested. I'll find another hotel. There must be one within driving distance."

"Ten miles away," Sir Andrew assured her. "And full up at this time of year. It's the holiday season, remember. Would you mind camping, Adam?"

"Not at all," Adam smiled. "It's very kind of you to offer. I'm sorry we're causing so much trouble. It didn't occur to me that there might be any problem finding a room.''

A lean, grizzled man with sandy greying hair was listening, his elbows on the bar. ''I'll get the tent down for you in a while, Andy,'' he said cheerfully. He smiled at Kit. ''Don't worry, we've done it before. People often drop in unexpectedly, and we keep the tent in the loft for that reason.'' He had a peculiar mixture of Canadian and Scottish accents, his voice a warm burr. ''I'm the landlord, for my sins—Tommy Macpherson. I came over to this country in 1939 to fight, and I never went back. My people came from Scotland originally, and I came up here for a holiday during the war and got bitten by the bug. So I bought this place after peace broke out, and settled down.''

''You're Canadian?'' asked Adam with interest.

''I was born in Canada, yes, in a place very like this—my father emigrated from Scotland during the depression. He was in the first war, of course, and never got a job afterwards, so he emigrated.''

''You must have been very young when you joined up,'' Kit said with sympathy.

Tommy Mac laughed, and his friends joined in noisily. He gave her a wink. ''I told them I was eighteen, but I was only just turned seventeen. My father was dead by then, and my mother had married again. I knew she would back me up if they wrote and asked how old I was—she was a tough woman. She knew I couldn't wait to get in on the fun.''

''I would have been worried sick,'' said Kit, shocked at the thought of such a young boy fighting in a war.

''I came through without a scratch until the last few months,'' Tommy Mac told her. ''Then I got this...''

He moved round from behind the bar and she saw that he limped. "My left leg...shot to pieces. They made me a fake one. It works well enough."

A small, thin woman came into the bar, stopped dead at sight of Kit and stared. "I was coming to say lunch was ready, boys," she said.

Tommy Mac introduced her. "My wife, Molly. She's a wonderful cook, so don't let the good food spoil. Go and enjoy your meal."

They ate at one large, oval table, helping themselves from a heated trolley at the side of the room. The meal began with a thick Scots broth, enriched with barley and pieces of ham, followed by lamb chops with new potatoes and peas, with trifle to finish the meal splendidly. The men stamped to and fro, transferring their empty plates to a second trolley and getting their next course. Kit offered to help Mrs. Macpherson with the washing up.

"We have a dish-washer, my dear," she was told. "We're thoroughly modernised here now—I saw to that."

"Tell you what," said Andy, "we'll go for a stroll along the river while your boss talks to George. He won't need you, will he?"

Adam stiffened. "I'm afraid I will need her," he said coldly. "She's here to work, not amuse herself."

Andy grimaced at Kit. "Slave-driver, eh?" he muttered to her under his breath.

Kit glared at Adam, who glared back, then turned to his host. "I suppose you all knew Jan Watowski, if you served in the same squadron?"

"Only for a while," Tommy Mac acknowledged. "The Poles formed their own squadron after a bit, and

Jan joined that. He'd come over here before the majority of them, you see, speaking English the way he did. He was the first to join up."

"I was in charge of that squadron, the Polish one," said George Loxford. "That was how I came to know Jan so well. I spoke some Polish—I picked it up at Oxford just before the war. I had a Polish professor tutoring me, and he taught me enough to get by in an emergency. It was damned useful later."

"Tell me about Jan Watowski," Adam invited.

George shrugged. "What can I say? He was a damn good flyer. A bit reckless, but we all were that at times. He had a sort of damn-your-eyes touchiness if he thought he was being got at . . . his temper was a bit hair-trigger, to be frank. He blew up at a moment's notice. But during the war years we all lived on our nerves, we were under so much strain. Jan didn't stand out in that respect."

"What about girls?" Adam asked.

They all laughed. Tommy Mac said, "Ah, now you're talking, but don't let Molly hear you! Look, old man, we were knee-deep in the other sex all the time. The RAF drew them like flies. The Poles had an additional glamour, of course, being foreigners."

"Jan was a handsome blighter, too. Off duty he always had a girl in tow," George grinned.

"Wasn't there one special one?"

"I wouldn't have said so," George frowned. "What are you getting at exactly? He was never married or engaged, anyway."

"According to Count Poniatowski you recommended some fishing village to Jan."

George grinned. "That's right, so I did. I'd forgotten about it." He glanced at Sir Andrew. "I told him about Coldmellow."

Sir Andrew sat up. "You never told me that! Did he go there?"

George nodded. "He got quite keen on the place. He enjoyed a spot of fishing. He used to pop off there whenever he had a few days off—stayed with some old hag in the village. She came to see me after Jan died, trying to get some money he owed her for his keep. I paid her off and gave her a flea in her ear. Jan had died for people like her. She made me sick."

"Coldmellow?" Adam repeated. "Where's that?"

"In Dorset," Sir Andrew told him. "I live there, actually."

Adam stared at him. "Do you indeed? That's useful. I would like to go down there and look around, try to find people who remembered Jan."

"I doubt if you will," said Andy. "I didn't know he'd ever been there, and I've lived in the village all my life. But you're welcome to come and stay with me any time you like." He looked at Kit eagerly. "You'll come, won't you?"

"We couldn't trouble you," Adam said icily.

"No trouble," said Andy. "I've got a barracks of a house. There are rooms galore. If you don't mind making your own beds and so on...can't get much help these days. I have a woman from the village every day and it takes her all her time to keep the house clean. I cook my own meals and make my own bed. Every little helps."

"Andy is the lord of the manor," said George Loxford with wry amusement. "Doesn't look the part, does he?" he said, eyeing Andy's ancient clothes.

"I farm my own land with the help of a couple of chaps. We run sheep on the downs. The land is chalk, you see. Can't grow much on it, but it does for sheep."

"I would love to stay with you," said Kit. "I'm sure my uncle would like to meet you. We'll show you round the studios."

They all stared at her. Adam said drily, "Kit's uncle is J.K. Ashley, the head of our company."

"Good lord," said Andy, impressed. "Would you really take me round the studios? That would be fantastic."

Kit laughed. "They're not as fascinating as they sound, but I'll be happy to show you round."

She was enjoying the way Andy looked at her, the admiration and appreciation in his blue eyes. He was an attractive young man, more or less her own age, and her ego had taken a battering in the last few days. It was a soothing experience to have a presentable young man look at one with such obvious interest, especially since she could see that Adam resented Andy's attentions to her.

Adam stood up restlessly. "Well, maybe we might take that walk now," he said.

"Fine," said Andy, seizing Kit's arm in a possessive grip. "Come on, the river looks marvellous with the sun on it . . ."

Adam angrily followed them from the room.

CHAPTER SIX

A FEW lean cows grazed calmly on the far side of the river. Midges danced beneath the trees, and hovered over the water, their flimsy wings transparent in the sunshine. A dragonfly darted up river in a flash of green.

"Pretty, isn't it?" Andy murmured.

She smiled round at him. "Beautiful. Look at those rushes! I just saw something hop through them."

"Frogs," Andy shrugged. "Dozens of them around at this time of the year. They've just spawned. At times the banks have strings of frogs-spawn drifting beside them. The local kids are always down here, blast them, muddying up the water and littering the place with jam jars."

Kit laughed. "Boys are the same everywhere."

"Too true. I have terrific problems with them at Coldmellow. I breed pheasants and the boys are always getting in the coverts and scaring hell out of the birds."

"Do you shoot the pheasants?" Kit asked regretfully. "They're such lovely-looking birds."

"Jolly-looking yes," Andy agreed. "I let the shooting rights, in fact. It all adds to my shrinking income. I've got a gamekeeper—good chap. He used to work in a factory and was desperate to get a job back on the land. He loves the work, particularly working with pheasants.''

"How do you breed them? I'm rather ignorant of country matters," said Kit.

Andy chuckled. "Do you read Shakespeare much? D'you know what he meant when he said country matters?" He winked at her, taking her hand. "He meant goings on in country lanes, kissing behind the hedge and so on... I was always puzzled by that bit in *Hamlet* until I saw it acted on the stage, and the chap playing Hamlet was pretty explicit..."

They talked about Shakespeare's delight in double meanings while they wandered along the river bank, watching the dazzle of light on the clear water, the slow sway of the weeds near the bank, the occasional dart of a fish from beneath his shady cover. The river had a clarity unusual in modern times of pollution, and Kit could understand why it exercised a spell on men's minds to sit in silence and throw out a lure to the lurking fish.

Andy told her how to breed pheasants, making her grimace at the picture of the young birds feeding on carrion, dead animals deliberately hung in the trees to rot so that maggots would breed in the flesh and provide plenty of food for the adult birds to find for their young.

"Disgusting, really, isn't it?" Andy agreed. "But it has to be done. Left to themselves the pheasant population would soon drop. We have to provide the carrion for them to feed on, you see."

"So you breed pheasants and sheep together?"

"Not really. The pheasants live in coverts, little copses fenced in to keep out kids. The sheep live out on the open downland."

Kit glanced backwards. Adam was a hundred feet behind, walking much slower with George Loxford, deep in conversation about Jan Watowski, but as she turned her head Adam's eyes met hers. He stared coldly at her hand, linked with Andy's, then looked up at her again. She gave him a sweet smile before turning back to ask Andy another question.

"You know, you're a wonderful listener," Andy told her eagerly. "Most girls chatter all the time, and are never interested in anything but clothes and pop music. It's marvellous to meet a girl who's interested in things."

"Your life is so fascinating," she said sincerely. "It must be wonderful to live in a rambling manor house surrounded by acres of downland and sheep and pheasants..."

"Well, obviously I like it," he said. "But it isn't everyone's idea of Paradise. Too much work attached. I'm up at dawn most days and working until it's dark, and even then I have a hundred jobs to do around the house. When you haven't much money you have to do your own repairs. I'm a pretty fair carpenter, plumber and electrician by now. I've learnt from experience and books. I once nearly burnt down the house with some faulty wiring, but I'm learning all the time."

"What's Coldmellow like?" she asked.

"Remote but very beautiful," he said proudly. "We've got a church, a pub and a few cottages. In winter that's all, but in summer the caravan camp opens up and we get some tourists. Not many, but it brings money to the village.''

"I wonder where Jan Watowski stayed?"

"I can't imagine. The pub, maybe. Although it isn't really a residential pub, just a tiny place. I think there are only three bedrooms. Maybe the landlord put him up, though."

"You say the fishing is good?"

"Pretty fair now, but according to my father it was great in the war because so few people came to fish it. Just the locals who knew the place. It's a trout river. I own the rights. I re-stock regularly, but we get a lot of poaching."

"I've never been fishing," Kit commented.

Andy grinned enthusiastically at her. "We must take you out with a rod when you come to stay. I can offer you a mount, too. I've got a couple of horses, both steady old hacks. You would be safe on either of them."

"I envy you your life," she sighed.

Andy looked amused. "Funny—I envy you yours. Now, we've talked about me for hours. How about you? Your life must be packed with excitement. What do you do exactly?"

She talked of her work and he listened, wide-eyed, asking her dozens of questions.

They reached an old stone bridge and walked on to it, leaning on the parapet to stare down into the dimpling water. The river chuckled as it ran over the pebbles on its bed, and a kingfisher flashed over the surface, striking and flapping away with a fish in its beak.

"Oh! How marvellous! How I wish I had a camera with me!" she said excitedly.

"You'd have to have a pretty good one to catch that," George Loxford told her as he and Adam joined them.

Adam glanced sidelong at Kit, who met his gaze defiantly, pleased that he should see the impression she had made on Andy.

Adam leaned on the bridge beside her. She stiffened, deeply aware of his lean muscled body close to her. His brown hands rested on the parapet, close touching her own. She felt a wave of unbearable weakness, a sensual longing foreign to her hitherto, and half closed her lids, swallowing. He shifted slightly. She was conscious of every breath he drew, every movement he made. Her heart quickened, her breath rasped in her throat.

"How clear the water is," she said huskily.

"There's that huge great blighter you're after, George," said Andy, darting to the other side of the bridge.

George followed and the two men peered down into the weedy depths.

"I'll get him one day," George said with determination. "He's a cunning brute..."

He and Andy moved down off the bridge and stood on the bank a little below, staring into the river, out of earshot.

Adam stared down without moving, watching the dancing glint of the sun on the river.

"You've made quite a hit with our young squire," he said suddenly, his tone acid.

"I like him, too," she retorted.

"You've made that obvious," Adam snapped. "A little too obvious."

"What's that supposed to mean?"

"All this flirtation is supposed to make me jealous, isn't it?" he drawled. "You've practically flung yourself at the boy. He must be getting the impression you've fallen hard at first sight. He'll have a cruel awakening when he realises you've been using him as a weapon to punish me with..."

This was too near the truth to be bearable. She flared at once, humiliated, defiant, hurt.

"Your vanity is colossal! I haven't been pretending to like Andy—I really like him. He's a very attractive man."

"Barely twenty-five and spends all day with sheep! An easy victim for you," Adam said bitingly.

"I find him charming," she said, "Good-looking, friendly, kind..."

"Just the sort of husband for an old-fashioned girl like you, I suppose?"

"Exactly," she said.

Adam turned his head and stared at her icily. "My God, women can be ruthless opportunists!"

"Not as ruthless as some men," she retorted.

"Well, I wish you luck with your fishing," Adam ground out. "The hook is very attractively baited, I grant you that, and I suspect the fish is already well and truly caught. I only hope you don't live to regret your catch."

Andy and George joined them, glancing at them curiously. "What was that about fishing?" Andy asked. "Do you want to do some while you're here, Adam?"

"I'm afraid we won't be here long enough," Adam said. "We must return to London tomorrow. I've learnt what I came here to learn."

"Thorough chaps, you television boys," George Loxford put in. "Coming all this way just to find out where Jan Watowski spent his weekends!"

"Oh, I learnt a lot more than that," Adam said curiously, glancing at Kit. "I learnt something about human nature, too."

She coloured and glanced away. She knew what he meant by that cryptic remark, and if he thought he would embarrass her he was wrong. She was proof against his sarcastic comments by now.

They walked back to the little whitewashed inn together, in a friendly group, talking about fishing. Tommy Mac limped to meet them, grinning. "Had a good time? I suppose George cursed the sunshine all the time? Never mind, George. The weather report on the radio just now said that it would rain tonight and probably tomorrow, so while there's life there's hope."

"Thank God for that," George groaned. "I mean to have another swipe at that great chap down near the bridge. I'll get him if it kills me..."

They had supper together in the pleasant, barely furnished little dining-room, a meal of the same simple, nourishing, filling variety as the lunch. Afterwards they played cards and Scrabble, then went up to bed very early.

From the window of her tiny, low-ceilinged room Kit watched Adam and Andy moving about around the battered Army surplus tent which had been pitched in the paddock in the shelter of a low stone wall. The horse came down, curious to inspect their behaviour, and Adam stroked his nose, offering him a lump of sugar.

He turned round suddenly and glanced at the upper storey of the inn, catching Kit unawares. There was still enough light to see by, and Kit saw the expression of Adam's face clearly enough. Her heart plummeted.

She dived away from the window and into bed, pulling the sheet up around her ears.

It was cruel of him to look at her like that. He made her knees turn to jelly. That hunger in his face was more than she could stand. He had no right to look at her like that when he refused to love where he desired. The two things had to go hand in hand, or not at all.

Towards dawn she woke from a deep sleep, reluctant to be torn from a dream of Adam, and heard the soft patter of rain on the river. The thatched roof rustled in a growing wind. She thought of Adam and Andy out there in the wind and rain, and grew anxious about them. Was that battered old tent really weatherproof?

She lay in her warm cocoon, drowsily thinking that they ought to come into the house, then drifted back to sleep without realising she was doing so, back to a dream in which Adam held her possessively in his arms and kissed her until she was limp and yielding, all her reservations forgotten in the sheer delight of his lovemaking.

She awoke to the resounding boom of a gong, and lay frowning for an instant, not remembering where she was, then jumped out of bed and looked out of her window.

It was still raining, a thin cold drizzle which danced on the river surface and made little pools on the paths leading from the house.

There was no sign of activity around the tent. The horse was hunched up against the leeward wall, his coat shining damply in the rain.

She dressed hastily and rushed downstairs. The men were all seated around the table, munching cereal. Glancing at her watch, she saw with horror that it was only seven.

"We like to get out early," said Tommy Mac with a grin.

"And we have to catch a train at ten," Adam told her. "There isn't another one until later tonight."

Andy sighed. "A pity you have to go, but I'm going home at the weekend. Will you come to stay then? We'll ferret around in the village for information."

"Andy will find out more than you ever could," George Loxford told them. "The people will talk to him where they wouldn't do to you. Very close, country people. They might be suspicious of you if you start asking questions."

Adam looked obstinate. "Oh, I always find people very helpful," he denied.

"Well, I would love to come and stay," Kit told Andy in a defiant mood. "Coldmellow sounds so fascinating. Thank you for inviting me."

"Marvellous!" Andy beamed at her. "I've just realised—it's the Country Club dance this weekend. Saturday night. Would you care to go? It can be quite an event, believe me! A good band, great food and everyone in the district goes to it. You'd meet most of the local people."

"Not the villagers," Adam said disagreeably. "They aren't likely to be present, I imagine."

Andy hesitated. "Well, no, perhaps not. But it's great fun, Kit. Do say you'll come!"

"I'd love to," she said.

Adam pushed his plate away and stood up. "I must pack. Are you packed, Kit?"

"It won't take long," she said.

"There's plenty of time," Andy demurred. "I'll drive you to the station. I say, why not stay a few days? It seems a waste of time to come all this way just for a few hours."

"Impossible," Adam said curtly. "We've got work to do in London."

Andy looked at Kit hopefully, but she shrugged and sighed. "I have to do as I'm told," she said, adding bitterly, "In working hours."

Adam gave her a cold look and left the room.

They made their goodbyes to the fishermen who were eager to get down to the river. Andy hung around to drive them, chatting to Kit while she packed her few belongings. "I say," he said, as he saw her Paris dress, "that's gorgeous. Will you wear it for the dance?"

"Of course I will," she promised. "It's nice, isn't it?"

"Lovely colour. I bet you look terrific in it." He gave her an admiring glance. "You're terrific even in jeans. Some girls look like elephants in jeans, but they suit you. You're so slender."

She smiled at him. "Thank you."

They drove to the station in one of the estate cars. The road was awash with water in places where the land dipped, and the estate car sometimes sent up showers of water which ran down the windows in muddy yellow streaks.

The stationmaster peered out at them in astonishment. "Going back so soon?" He nodded to Andy. "It is yourself, Sir Andrew. Are you off away to London with them?"

"Not yet," Andy said cheerfully. "I'm here until Saturday."

"Won't you be too tired for a dance after a journey like that?" Adam asked him disagreeably.

Andy laughed. "Not me! I could dance with Kit even if I was just back from the moon."

Adam gave her a nasty look and said nothing. The train came into view. Andy sighed. "It's here already. That's a pity."

They stowed their luggage into a compartment and jumped on board. Kit smiled at Andy. "I'll see you again soon, then."

Emboldened, he jumped up on the running board and kissed her rapidly on the mouth just as the train began to move again. Looking back with a smile, she saw him staring after them, waving. She waved back until he was out of sight, then sank back into her window seat.

"Very touching," Adam said harshly. "You've progressed a long way in twenty-four hours, haven't you? You only met him yesterday and already he's kissing you goodbye. Congratulations. You're a fast worker, I'll say that for you."

"Oh, shut up!" she said, curling up in her corner to doze.

SHE went into the office next day to do some work on another long-term project, a programme about British scientific achievements for which she was doing one insert. There was no hurry over this. The rest of the programme was still being researched, and her own small item had been scripted by a scientist based at Oxford who was never available when she tried to make arrangements to see him.

Today she rang him again, was fobbed off by his secretary, a brittle icicle of a woman who behaved as if her boss was God Almighty, and expected everyone else to treat him with the same adoration.

Irritated, Kit doodled on her pad for a while, wondering how she was ever going to get the interview. Adam strolled in a moment later, eyeing her coldly.

"Busy as usual, I see."

"I've just been trying to get through to Doctor Lombard. I'm beginning to think he only talks to the Archangel Gabriel."

"Who's handling the rest of that? Donald Meakin? Right, I'll get Don on to Lombard. I expect he'll talk to Don."

"I see. It's my sex which has bedevilled my attempts to see him, is it? What chauvinism!"

"I doubt if it's Lombard himself," Adam said. "More likely his secretary fends off all females."

"That figures," Kit agreed.

"In matters of chauvinism," Adam said sarcastically, "I find women far worse offenders than men."

"I'm sure you do," Kit snapped. "But you can always turn on the old Rothbury charm, can't you? And watch the little birds fall off their twigs into your waiting hands?"

"As you did?" His voice had an edge to it.

"I'm immunised," she said.

"Are you?" He strolled closer.

Kit backed, alarmed by his nearness, her pulses beginning to thunder. "Adam..."

"What?" he asked silkily. "Why the sudden panic? I thought you were immune to my so-called charm?"

"Why don't you leave me alone?" Her voice was fraught with nerves.

"Perhaps I find that well-nigh impossible," Adam said on a sudden note of sincerity. His eyes ate her face hungrily. "You're lovely, Kit..."

"No, Adam," she said weakly as he reached for her, but her protest was lost as his mouth came down over hers. She put up her hands to push him away, but when they touched his broad shoulders they clung despairingly, creeping round his neck to touch the thick dark hair on the back of his head. She abandoned pretence, and curved in against him, pressing herself against the muscled hardness of his chest, aching for the feel of him. Their parted lips clung hotly, sending shivers of pleasure down her spine, and she moaned softly.

He drew back, looking down at her, the closed lids, the moist mouth and upturned features.

She opened her eyes reluctantly. "You're a bastard," she whispered.

"Now say you're immune," answered Adam fiercely. "When young Lochinvar from Coldmellow takes you to the ball, kiss him and try to forget me. I hope you find every second in his company complete hell..."

"I thought you weren't jealous," she said on a sigh.

"You knew damned well I was," Adam told her bitterly. "I detest that young oaf."

"He isn't! He's charming."

"I'd like to hold him under his own river until he drowns," Adam ground out.

"Adam! What a rotten thing to say!"

He caught her by the shoulders and shook her. "Do you think I'm going to enjoy seeing you flirt with him under my nose, watch you dancing in his arms, see him kiss you and gaze at you like a moonstruck calf? The very thought of it sends me mad!"

She looked at him from under her lashes soberly. "You have a dog-in-the manger attitude, haven't you?"

"I want you," he groaned. "God, Kit, how I want you!"

"But not enough," she said.

"I've told you why," he said, almost pleadingly. "Kit, if you could only understand...the very thought of marriage makes my blood run cold. It petrifies me."

"I'm sorry," she said gently. "I do understand. Look, Adam, forget it. We'll go our separate ways and each live the life we have to live. I'll find the man for me one day. Maybe it's Andy—I don't know. He's attractive enough. Probably if you weren't around in my life I would be in love with him now. He's just the sort of man I've always wanted to marry. We understand each other, talk the same language, and I think I could love him."

"God," he groaned, releasing her and turning away. "Kit, stop it! You're torturing me."

"I didn't mean to," she assured him. "I hate to hurt you. But you keep bringing it up—as you did just now."

"God help me, I can't leave you alone," he said thickly. "I've never been in love before, I think. Nothing like this. I've known you for years at a distance. I was used to you. Then suddenly my eye seemed to take you in... I think I fell in love with you the day we flew to Paris. Or that was when I began to realise it—I don't know. You looked round at me and smiled and I felt a sort of ache start up inside me."

She was trembling. "You said you weren't in love, Adam. You told me it wasn't love you felt ..."

"I lied, damn you. Of course I lied. I didn't want to believe it. I didn't want to love you. Love is a trap and a nightmare. I always knew it would be, and that's just how I've found it. Since knowing I loved you I've lived in hell."

She looked at his dark face with a curious sort of pity. "Poor Adam. What a shame!"

"Don't patronise me, woman!" he shouted. "I'm not a total wreck yet. I still have my pride and I won't be pitied."

She sighed. "We have nothing to say to each other, Adam, have we? It would be best to stop seeing each other. I'll ask J.K. to transfer me to another department."

"You will not!" Adam turned on her furiously. "When I want you transferred I'll do the asking."

"It would be better for both of us," she protested.

"If I can stand it, you can," Adam ground out.

"But if it's making you miserable, Adam?"

He turned away impatiently. "I'll find consolations."

"No doubt," she said, her own jealousy leaping up. "You've found them before, haven't you, Adam?"

He slammed out of the room without answering.

CHAPTER SEVEN

KIT was grateful to find herself snowed under with work next day, when Don Meakin contrived somehow to fix up the necessary interview with Dr. Lombard. Since the Doctor was so busy it was arranged that she should go down there with a camera unit and film the interview at once, with only a brief rehearsal.

"Won't he need time to mock up a skeleton script?" she asked Don doubtfully. "It's a very complex subject he's dealing with—frankly I didn't understand a word I read on it."

Don laughed and pinched her chin. "Honey, Lombard is the only man in the world who knows anything about it, believe me! He has it all at his fingertips. Just try to keep him within the time limit. That will be a big enough job, I can tell you. Once he's riding his hobbyhorse nothing can stop him."

"I hope he isn't as unapproachable as his secretary," she sighed faintly.

Don grinned. "No one could be that unapproachable! I met the lady, and my word! Talk about fish fingers! She is pure ice from head to toe. The only time she thaws out is when her boss talks to her."

"Adam suspected it might be like that," Kit said, finding it pleasurable just to say his name.

"Adam should know," Don murmured. "Every secretary he ever had fell like a ton of bricks."

Kit stiffened. She might have guessed!

She enjoyed her meeting with Dr. Lombard, as it turned out, because he was far more friendly than she had anticipated, and showed the fascinated professional interest in her job which she usually found among people who also had interesting work. Dr. Lombard asked her searching questions, inspected the cameras, the wiring, the electronic gadgets, tirelessly questioned the camera crew and was eager to learn all he could about the whole subject.

When it came to the actual interview she was relieved to find how rapidly he picked up what she wanted. They worked out a series of questions which would lead him into the necessary explanations without presenting the viewer with a slab of information he could not understand.

"We have to break it up," she explained to Dr. Lombard. "It's assimilated easier in small doses."

He nodded. "I understand. I've often wondered why it was done like that."

She smiled. "We're aiming the series at the general public, not scientists like yourself. People like to know about these things, but as we're aiming at so wide a mixture of audiences, we have to be careful how we present it."

They ran through the interview in rehearsal, then broke for coffee and talked over what had not come through too well, seeking ways of simplifying the information. Then they did the interview again for real. Dr. Lombard was much better the second time, far more relaxed and human. Kit was pleased with the way things had gone.

"That was splendid, Dr. Lombard," she told him warmly. "Thank you so much for your time and trouble...I hope you'll be able to look in when the series starts. We'll let you know in advance when it's scheduled."

He smiled at her, his face already becoming abstracted once more. "Thank you, thank you, Miss..."

His secretary, who had turned out to be comparatively young and attractive, gave Kit an icy smile. "I'll see you out, Miss Ashley," she said pointedly.

Amused, Kit allowed herself to be shepherded out of the room. She was a nuisance, she gathered, who had wasted the great man's valuable time.

That evening, she amused J.K. by recounting the anecdote, with a brief mimicry of the secretary's glacial expression, and of Doctor Lombard's swift loss of interest once he had sucked in all the knowledge he could acquire of television procedures.

"He's a brilliant man, but my word, he's maddening!"

"Worse than Adam?" asked J.K. slyly.

She flushed and wished for the hundredth time that she could control her reactions.

"How is Adam?" J.K. enquired, watching her with a little frown. "How did the trip to Scotland go?"

"I think he found out what he wanted to know," she said.

"What's he up to? Do you think there's a secret in Watowski's life that Landell suppressed?"

She shrugged. "It's possible. Certainly Landell was hostile when we visited him, and why should he be otherwise?"

"It could just be Adam's effect on him," J.K. pointed out shrewdly. "Adam has been known to put people's backs up, hasn't he, darling?"

She met his gaze squarely. "Me, you mean? I think that's different."

"Oh? Why?" asked J.K. softly.

She sighed. "Adam is an old-fashioned chauvinist, you know. He sees women as pets and playthings, never as equals, and that can be infuriating."

"I see," said J.K.

She met his shrewd, clear-sighted stare and wondered uneasily just what he did see—with her uncle you could never be sure. He saw much more than one would wish. She twisted away restlessly and fiddled with the curtain, staring out of the window at the garden.

"We're both going down to Dorset this weekend," she said.

"Dorset? Why Dorset? This habit of tearing off alone together is surprising, Kit. What is going on between you two?"

"We're still on the Watowski trail," she assured him. "This time we're looking for someone in a village called Coldmellow." She explained how they had heard about Watowski's visits to the village, and described Sir Andrew.

"He sounds charming," J.K. commented.

"He is," she agreed.

J.K. watched her. "Did Adam like him?"

Kit turned and met his eyes defiantly. "Not much."

"Hmm ... interesting."

Kit did not enquire what he meant. She preferred not to know. Instead, she asked if he would like some more coffee, poured both him and herself some, and settled down to talk about Scotland.

She saw nothing of Adam during that week. Either he was busy or he was avoiding her. She cared little which it was—the absence of his constant watchfulness was a relief. It gave her time to absorb the impact of their relationship, gave her time to consider her own position, to know for certain that she was not prepared to go into a tormenting sexual relationship which could only end in misery.

Edward rang her several times, but she pleaded pressure of work to escape him. She sensed from his attitude that he knew that there was little hope in pursuing their friendship. Edward was not in love with her. She had been a pleasant, attractive companion, nothing more, and her relationship with J.K. had been of stronger importance to Edward than herself.

On Friday evening, as she was towelling her hair vigorously after washing it, the phone rang. She answered it irritably, half expecting it to be Edward again.

It was Andy, his voice sounding very muffled, as though he was speaking under water.

"Oh, hello," she said warmly. "Where are you?"

"Still in Scotland," he said. "This is a dreadful line. Can you hear me?"

"Yes, very well, but you do sound strange ..."

"You sound like a deep sea diver," he said.

She laughed. "How did the fishing go?"

"Wonderful! We've been feeding off salmon every night! I'm just off to catch the night train down to London. I'll be there around breakfast time. I suppose you wouldn't meet me?"

His eagerness made her smile. "Of course I will. Why not have breakfast at my flat?"

"Could I? That's very decent of you. Are you sure it will be no trouble?"

"It would be fun," she said firmly. "You turned out of your bed for me. Providing your breakfast seems little enough in return."

When he had rung off she finished drying her hair, blow-drying it at the end with her hand-dryer so that it fell into the usual little tight curls. She had always been grateful that her hair curled naturally. It saved a fortune in hairdresser's bills, and the short style suited her face.

She went into the kitchenette, wearing a wraparound cotton robe, and began to make herself a simple supper of salad and cold meat.

Suddenly the doorbell rang, making her jump. She glanced at her watch. J.K.? She went back to the door, opened it and stiffened at the sight of Adam.

He was leaning on the door frame, casually dressed in a black sweater and jeans, his lean face expressionless.

"What do you want?" she asked with hostility.

"We haven't made arrangements for tomorrow," he said, glancing past her. "Aren't you going to ask me in?"

"No," she said directly. "I'm not dressed for visitors."

He let his cool glance drift over her robe. "That seems to cover the subject pretty thoroughly."

She flushed, drawing the edges of it closer together. "Surely you could have rung?"

"I could have done," he said flatly. "I didn't." His attitude was one of determination, and she hesitated, then shrugged.

"Oh, very well..." She stood back and he passed her into the flat.

He flung himself down into a chair, leaned his head back and closed his eyes briefly.

He looked suddenly deathly tired. The fine bones of his face were standing out beneath his skin, his mouth had a weary look, as if he had not slept. Kit felt a pricking of compassion for him.

"Would you like some coffee?" she asked quietly.

He opened his eyes and looked at her, the grey eyes wide. "Thank you. Yes."

She moved into the kitchen. After a moment Adam followed and leaned against the wall, watching her. She found his gaze unbearable.

"You look tired. Why don't you go back into the sitting-room and relax?"

"I'm fine," he said in flat tones.

"You don't look it."

"For God's sake, Kit!" His explosion was harsh and took her by surprise.

She bit her lip and was silent. The percolator began to bubble. She moved about, laying out cups and getting cream from the fridge. Once she had to pass Adam to get the sugar bowl from a cupboard. He did not move aside, so she had to lean past him, almost touching him, every nerve in her body aware of him.

At such close quarters she saw the lines around his mouth and eyes, touched with weariness and pain, and the tension implicit in his taut mouth and jaw.

She went back across the room, conscious of a burning need to touch him, to feel the hardness of his chest under her hands, the width of his shoulders inviting her caress.

"Cream and sugar?" she asked politely.

"Cream, no sugar," he said curtly.

She poured the coffee, added cream to his and passed him the cup. "Shall we go and sit down?"

He glanced at her tray, laid for one. "Are you going to eat your supper?"

She looked at it, too. "There is enough for two. Would you like some?"

He shook his head. "No thanks. I'm not hungry."

"Neither am I," she said.

Wryly, he said, "You apparently were until I arrived."

She walked through into the little sitting-room and sat down with her coffee. Adam followed and leaned against the window, staring out at the twilit sky. The London skyline was etched in darkly against a lavender-washed horizon. The street lights were coming on and the traffic sounded subdued.

"It's quiet here," he murmured. "You have a charming flat."

"It's very expensive," she sighed. "The rent went up twice in the last year."

He turned back, sipping his coffee slowly. He looked toweringly tall in the little room, making her feel helpless beside him.

"Have you heard from your young Lochinvar?" he asked suddenly, surprising her.

Kit flushed. "He rang just now."

"Is he back?" Adam watched her closely.

"No, he's on his way now. I'm meeting him tomorrow morning and giving him breakfast."

"Here?" Adam glanced round the room, eyes narrowed, as if he saw it for the first time.

"Yes, here." She knew she sounded defiant, but she no longer cared. Why was he here, why was he standing there like that, as tense as a leopard about to pounce?

"Very intimate," Adam drawled unpleasantly.

She flushed. "No more so than this..."

His eyes flashed to her face, narrowing, and she felt the colour rise hotly in her cheeks. After a long, harrowing pause Adam said, "Perhaps I should join you. We might as well go down to Dorset together in my car."

She shrugged. "As you please."

"The idea doesn't appeal to you?" He was acid in the enquiry, his expression grim.

"You don't like Andy," she pointed out. "If you're here there'll be a blight on the atmosphere."

"I'll cramp your style, you mean? You might not be able to flirt with young Dudley if I was around to watch?"

She glared at him. "We were just going to have a friendly meal together. If you insist on coming it won't be very friendly, will it?"

"I didn't notice my presence interfering with your flirtation in Scotland," he said disagreeably, putting down his empty cup.

"Oh, Adam, stop it!" she burst out.

He walked to the door. "All right," he said in a grim voice. "I'll pick you and your boy-friend up at eleven o'clock tomorrow morning. We should be down in Dorset by two, or if we stop for lunch, around three."

The door slammed behind him. Kit sat very still for a moment, shivering, then picked up the coffee cups and took them into the kitchen to wash them. Then she went to bed, too miserable to eat or do anything but dive under the bedclothes and brood.

She was at the station next morning to meet Andy, as arranged. The train was dead on time, and she saw him hurrying along the platform towards her, first among the crowd of descending passengers, a huge leather grip in one hand, the other clutching a leather case of fishing equipment from which protruded rods.

He grinned happily when he saw her. "You're here! I was afraid you would forget!"

She laughed. "I'm not that absent-minded. We'll take a taxi, shall we? I didn't bring my car. It's impossible to park around here at this time of the morning."

Andy said, "This is very good of you. I'm awfully grateful."

"It's a pleasure," she said.

They took a taxi and arrived at her flat within twenty minutes. Andy stared at the house admiringly. "Lucky you to live in a place like this. I often wish I lived in London. Dorset can be very quiet. There's so much more to do up here."

"After work I'm often too tired to do anything," she groaned. "I wonder why it is that the grass is often greener on the other side of the fence? I envy you your quiet country life, I really do. I often wish I lived somewhere peaceful."

"You may do just that one day," said Andy, smiling at her. "If you married a farmer, for instance..."

Kit laughed, ushering him into her flat. "Who knows? Would you like to wash? Travelling all night makes one feel very grimy."

Andy vanished gratefully into the bathroom, while she went into the kitchen to get breakfast. The smell of bacon lured Andy there some time later. He sniffed the air hungrily.

"Delicious! I'm ravenous."

She gestured to the small table set for two. "Start on some cereal. Or would you like orange juice?"

"Cereal, thanks," he said. "What about you?"

She dished up the bacon and eggs. "I'll just have orange juice. I don't eat a big breakfast."

"I'm afraid I do," he confessed cheerfully, pouring milk on to cornflakes.

While he ate bacon and eggs later, he glanced at her, his brown skin flecked with round freckles like those on the shell of a brown hen's egg, his blue eyes very bright against his tan.

"Tell me, what is the situation between you and Rothbury?" he suddenly asked, taking her by surprise.

Kit was fiddling idly with the toast rack, and her hand jerked in shock. She looked at him questioningly. "He's my boss. He runs the department I work for..."

"Sure, I know that," he nodded. "I meant personally."

"Personally?"

Andy smiled gravely at her. "Oh, come on! I'm not dumb, you know. It sticks out a mile that there's something between you two. He watches you."

"Does he?" She looked down at her hand absently, picked up a piece of toast, buttered it. "There's nothing to tell," she said.

"Does that mean I'm intruding on private territory, or do you really mean that there's nothing to know?" he questioned acutely.

She spread marmalade carefully. "I mean that the situation is too complicated to explain. I'm not even sure I know myself."

"There is something, then? I thought so."

Kit grimaced wryly. "Something—or nothing."

"Is the complication on his side or yours?" Andy pressed.

Kit looked up at him, biting her lip. "On his," she admitted frankly.

Andy nodded with a sigh. "Married, is he?"

Kit laughed bitterly. "Oh, not that!"

Andy stared at her, then asked, "Look, you don't have to answer this, but are you in love with him?"

Feeling like a swimmer plunging into icy waters, Kit gave a little gasp of shock, then said faintly, "I'm not sure . . . perhaps . . . yes . . ."

Andy pushed away his plate. "Hence the big welcome I got?" He stared at her calmly, blue eyes clear as a summer sky. "You were using me as a smoke screen or a stick to beat him with?"

"Not exactly," she said miserably. "I'm sorry . . . I like you a lot. Really. I liked you at once, and you seemed to like me. If Adam didn't exist I would still have wanted to see you today, you know."

"But he does exist," said Andy.

She bent her head. "Yes." She looked up again, shamed. "Look here, do you want to back out of this weekend business? Adam will be here soon to drive us down to Dorset. If you want to forget it, just say so..."

"Why should I?" Andy asked her. "As you said, I like you. I knew from the start that there was something between the two of you. It was obvious that whatever it was had gone wrong, so I saw my chance and nipped in. I'm not complaining, just getting things straight. I know, and you know I know. So now we're all square and can go on from there."

She smiled at him. "You're very nice."

"So are you," he told her. "Can I have some of that toast? I'm still hungry."

She laughed and passed the toast rack.

Andy crunched a piece while he gazed out of the window. "This is a very nice flat. Have you lived here long?"

She told him while she cleared the table. He came back and offered to wash up, an offer she gratefully accepted. They worked together chattering cheerfully, and were laughing at a joke Andy told her when the doorbell rang.

"That will be Adam," Kit said, sobering.

Andy caught her hand and squeezed it. "Don't look so fed up. I'm on your side, whatever the problem is!"

She laughed, touched by his friendliness, and went to the door. Adam looked casually elegant in a suede jacket and fine cord trousers, his shirt open at the neck.

"Ready?" he asked coolly.

"Come in, we're almost ready."

He followed her in, glanced at Andy, who was standing in the kitchen doorway with a large blue striped apron tied around his waist. "Doing domestic work, Dudley?" Adam asked.

"Paying for my breakfast," Andy replied cheerfully. He stripped off the apron and went off to the bathroom while Kit vanished into the bedroom to collect her case, packed ready over night.

Moments later they were all in Adam's car heading for the motorway. It was a difficult journey. Adam was distinctly cool all the way. Kit and Andy sat in the back, making strained conversation, always aware of Adam's brooding presence.

They stopped at Salisbury for lunch at a little pub in the market square, then drove on to Dorset.

"Why is your village called Coldmellow?" Kit asked.

"It's on a hill, hence the adjective Cold," Andy said. "And the family who owned it in the middle ages were called Meleau, later corrupted to Mellow. They vanished from the scene during the Elizabethan age. My family arrived on it in the eighteenth century. My ancestor was an Indian Nabob, one of the chaps who worked for the East India Company and made a fortune out of taxing the natives. He came back home with his ill-gotten gains, bought the manor and all the titles that went with it and started a dynasty. His grandson was knighted during the reign of George the Fourth because he was around on some royal visit."

"Are there any stories about Coldmellow? Any ghosts or murders worth recording?"

"There's supposed to be a ghost that haunts the church, no one knows why, but some people think it was a barn owl who lived in the tower. Murders?" Andy shrugged. "We're a law-abiding community."

"An undistinguished place, evidently," Adam commented.

Andy was not put out. "Oh, dull as ditchwater," he agreed. "You turn off here beside the school and take the lane which forks to the right."

Adam swung the car down the narrow lane, keeping a steady twenty miles an hour as he inched forward between hedges of pink may and waist-high flowers of wild parsley, foaming like detergent in the ditches.

As they crawled along they heard the sounds of the countryside through the open windows; the high sweet calls of blackbird and thrush, the cooing of a wood pigeon, the rustle of long grass in the wind.

"Look," Andy said. "Up there...Coldmellow village. See the spire?"

Through a fringe of dark green oaks they saw the spire ascend the sky, creamy stone fretting the bright blue.

"The river Mellow falls down the hillside as a stream," Andy said. "It widens at the bottom here. There it is, across that pasture..."

Peering out of the car, she saw a field of biscuit-coloured Jersey cows and, beyond them, the river bank, tree-lined and tranquil. The field was full of bright yellow buttercups and tall thistles. An elm stood sentinel at one end.

"My house is the first on the left," Andy told Adam. "You'll see the gates. Painted blue..."

Soon they had passed the blue gates and were moving up a wide driveway, lined on one side by a tall hedge of privet, with a line of lime trees on the other.

"We call this the Lime Tree Walk," Andy said. "It was planted by my great-grandfather. It's only just reached its peak. Planting trees is a patient occupation. You rarely live to see the fruits of your labour."

They swung round in front of the house. Curiously Kit stared up at it. Andy watched her, rather than the house.

Shabby, rambling, endearingly solid, it stood four-square to the winds blowing up the hill, a red brick Queen Anne edifice with white-pained sash windows and an uneven moss-starred red roof. Ivy clung to the bricks and sprawled from one side of the house to the other. Pink rose bushes flanked the front door, their blooms nodding to and fro.

A dog came galloping round the house, tail wagging furiously, barking a welcome.

Andy jumped out and received a rapturous greeting. On his knees, hugging the dog, he turned to grin at Kit as she joined him.

"This is Samson. He's a noisy brute."

The sleek red setter turned his attention to her, licking her hands as she stroked his fine coat.

"Shall we go in?" Andy asked. "We'll have to make our own tea, I'm afraid. Mrs. Hobbett will have gone home by now. She only comes in to do what she calls the 'heavy work', and she'll be back home at this time of day."

"I'll make the tea," Kit offered. "Just show me the kitchen."

"No, no," Andy protested, but she insisted, and he took her through into the large, starkly furnished kitchen. He left her while he showed Adam his room. Kit rummaged around, found a kettle and put it on the great black kitchen range. Then she found bread in a white bread bin, began to slice it thinly.

When Andy returned he found the kitchen table set for tea—a plate of bread and butter, some small queen cakes which she had found in a cake tin, jam, fish paste and honey. Kit was boiling eggs and laying out cups and saucers, her face intent.

Andy watched her for a moment, then as she turned and smiled at him he beamed. "You look at home already!"

"I feel it," she agreed, dimpling. "Do you want one egg or two?"

"I won't be a pig," Andy said. "One."

"Why not have two if you want them?" She waited, spoon poised to add another brown speckled egg to the saucepan.

Andy came across and seized her round the waist, smiling down at her, his blue eyes bright. "You gorgeous, surprising girl! I'm going to have to kiss you or burst . . ."

She laughed at his expression, and he kissed her on her nose, then quickly on her mouth.

As she drew back she heard a sound in the doorway. Adam stood there, his hands clenched at his sides in tight fists. His eyes were black with rage.

CHAPTER EIGHT

AFTER tea Kit went up to her room to settle in, unpack her clothes and get herself ready for the Country Club dance to which Andy was taking her. She left Adam and Andy washing up in a grim silence which alarmed her. Adam had been watchfully silent all through the meal, indeed.

Once unpacked, she found the bathroom, took a long relaxing bath and then went back to her room to press her dress. It took her some time to make various other preparations, and it was getting late by the time she was ready to leave.

She came down to find the two men waiting for her, both wearing evening suits.

Her glance flicked over Adam, taking in his formal attire and unsmiling features with a bitter-sweet pleasure. He stared back at her unyielding.

Andy was bubbling with delight, on the other hand. He seized her hand and made her twirl round, her skirts flying in a silky swish.

"You'll be the belle of the ball! What a fantastic dress! It looks even better on you than it did in your wardrobe."

She laughed. "I should hope so!"

"You'll be swamped by partners," Andy said regretfully. "Now, you must promise to save me at least

six dances! I'm taking you, after all." He glanced at
Adam. "Adam and I are taking you," he conceded.

"Don't mind me," said Adam disagreeably.

"Don't you dance?" asked Andy hopefully.

Adam stared at Kit. "I might do," he said. "But I'll
find my own partners."

Kit turned away. Andy took her arm and led her out
to the car. Adam followed more slowly. Kit was irritated with him. He was behaving like a sulky child.
Dog in the manger, she thought bitterly. And he talks
about being an adult!

The dance was being held in a large house set in a
park. The trees along the drive were strung with fairy
lights, red, white and blue, which gave a magical air to
the dark blue sky arching overhead. The car park was
already jammed with cars. They only just managed to
squeeze into it.

When they entered the ballroom they stood for a
while watching the dancers. Great crystal chandeliers
glittered from the ornate ceiling. The room was long
and lined with gilded mirrors which redoubled the effect of the throng. Distracting glimpses of naked arms
and shoulders, glittering diamonds, men's black
jackets, flashed at them from all sides in the reflected
images.

They were greeted by a tall, statuesque woman in
dark green who stared curiously at Kit when Andy introduced her as "a friend from London".

Andy persuaded Kit to dance almost at once. "Before the rush sets in," he flattered.

"I'm sure there won't be any rush," she demurred,
but accepted, and was swung into the moving crush in
a second.

Looking back, she saw Adam standing beside a window. He was looking extraordinarily handsome tonight, she thought. Evening dress suited him. It gave distinction to his features. His height and muscled fitness looked well in the dark cloth. His smooth black hair was brushed down, his grey eyes steely under the brilliant light from the chandeliers.

Andy began to whisper in her ear descriptions of the people he saw, telling her scandalous stories about them which she was sure he was inventing to amuse her.

As the music came to a crashing end, she turned and found herself face to face with a slim blonde girl in ice-blue who gave her a distinctly unpleasant look.

"Oh, hello, Anthea," Andy said uneasily.

"Hello," drawled the other girl. Her pale blue eyes flickered towards Kit enquiringly.

Andy introduced them. "This is Anthea Gable, Kit. She lives at Coldmellow, and runs our local riding school."

Kit smiled. Anthea nodded recognition but did not return the smile. She was an attractive girl, with regular features marred only by coldness.

"You come from London?" she asked, managing to make the question sound like an accusation.

Kit nodded, "Yes." The monosyllable was all she could force out. Anthea's hostility was too overpowering.

"Kit is a television producer," Andy said proudly.

Suddenly Kit knew the reason for Anthea's dislike and Andy's uneasiness. Andy had not mentioned another girl, but here, she knew for certain, was the girl whom he had carefully avoided mentioning. Anthea could only see her as a rival if she herself wanted Andy. Sharply, Kit considered Andy's face. Was he not interested in Anthea, or was he playing a more devious game?

"How fascinating," Anthea drawled, looking incredulous. "Really? I would never have guessed."

"We don't wear any uniforms," Kit said, irritated by the other girl's obvious disbelief.

"You look rather young for that sort of job," Anthea told her sweetly.

"Kit's uncle runs the studios," Andy informed her.

"Oh, I see," Anthea smiled, even more sweetly. That explains it, her expression said silently.

Adam had forced a way through to join them. He turned upon Anthea the full force of the Rothbury charm. She's just his sort of girl, thought Kit bitterly. Tall, slim, blonde—with model statistics and that frozen expression they all wear.

Anthea was thawing now, though, her blue eyes warming as she took in Adam's looks and airs of distinction.

"A television producer? How fantastic," she breathed, fluttering her long, false eyelashes at him. There was no note of disbelief in her voice now, only awe and flattery.

The music started up again. Adam's hand slid around Anthea's waist, and she smiled up at him coyly as they moved away. Over her blonde head Adam's eyes met Kit's stare. His face was coolly enigmatic. She could not guess what he was thinking now. Andy was urging her to dance again. She turned and smiled at him, dragging her thoughts away from Adam with difficulty.

From then on the evening became a succession of dances with Andy and his many friends. As he had prophesied Kit found herself much in demand. Her job was passport enough, but the effect of this London glamour was emphasised by her appearance, by the silky allure of her dress and her expensive French perfume. For once she looked the part of a TV producer. Ironically she wondered what these eager young men would think if they saw her working in her old jeans and sweaters, her muddy wellingtons squelching across a ploughed field in the making of some documentary, or swathed in the protection of an old duffle coat on a raw winter morning filming in empty dawn streets to avoid the complications of rush hour traffic in London. Her present garb was hardly representative. Most of her colleagues would not recognise her.

She thought of Joe, her favourite cameraman, his clever face absorbed as he clambered up for a good vantage point, dressed in crumpled jeans, his face smudged with London grime from walls or roofs. A nostalgic yearning for shop talk came over her as she chattered lightly to Dorset farmers who knew nothing of her world. I'm an alien here, she thought. I am the outsider. But then she always was, she sighed. She was looking in from outside all the time. The television camera was a great eye, constantly prying on other lives, and those behind it were an extension of it, seeing life through its wide crystal lens, trying to squash the untidy bulges of human activity into the square context of the television screen. There was a tendency to lop off offending limbs and branches, to simplify the rambling structures they observed. Human beings are more various and more unpredictable than the square world of television can comprehend. They refuse to be contained. They sprawl outwards in all directions.

"A penny for them," Andy asked her, seeing how quiet she had become.

She laughed. "My thoughts aren't worth a penny."

"You were frowning horribly," he told her. "They must have been nasty thoughts."

"Just sober ones," she sighed. To Joe she might have opened out, talked about her thoughts, but she shied away from discussing them with Andy somehow, although she sensed that he was intelligent enough to follow the trend of them, to see the problem facing the producer asked to make any aspect of human life simple. Anyone who has to select this aspect rather than another to present to the public has a huge problem on their hands. Whatever they put in or leave out they will be accused of bias or incompetence. It is in the nature of selection that someone will be offended by it.

"I'm very sober," Andy said comically. "I haven't touched strong drink all evening."

She laughed up at him. "Poor Andy! What a shame!"

Beyond his shoulder she saw Adam with Anthea's blonde head close to his cheek. Adam's steely gaze pierced her, sending a shiver of pain to her heart. As she watched he deliberately let his lips brush Anthea's hair, a caress which made the other girl turn to smile at him. Someone ought to warn Anthea against him, Kit thought bitterly. A man like Adam ought to wear a label—strictly for fun, no future prospects.

The crystal chandeliers danced glitteringly overhead, the girls in their pretty dresses swished to and
fro, their young men in attendance. The music swirled
on and on, the room grew warmer and warmer.

Andy took her out to supper in the long, cool supper room, where the tables were laid with salad bowls,
plates of cold chicken and ham, rolls, tiny sandwiches, great dishes of warm paella and a selection of
rich gâteaux or trifle.

"What will you have?" Andy enquired. "A little of
everything?"

"Just salad and chicken," she thanked him. "I'm
too warm to eat."

"Stifling in there, isn't it?" he agreed.

While he was gone she was surrounded with young
men, eager to chat her up in his absence, teasing,
flirting, flattering her, while she received glacial looks
from some of the local girls abandoned for her sake by
their boy-friends. It would have been a heady experience had she been heartwhole, but she was sick with
longing for Adam, and could not enjoy her unusual
popularity.

"Hey, you piratical collection, shove off!" Andy
said with indignation, returning with two brimming
plates. "I brought the lady, remember!"

"Don't be so selfish," one of them retorted. "She's
staying with you, you lucky devil!"

"Why are you staying with Andy?" asked one,
more straightforward than the rest. "Not making a
film about him, are you?"

The others all laughed, amused by this notion.
Andy bristled. "Why not? I'm a potential film star. I
always knew I would break into films one day..."

"Seriously, are you going to make a film around here?" asked the first young man seriously.

"We're researching the life of Jan Watowski, the Polish war poet," Kit said.

"Who?" asked one.

"Polish what?" asked another.

"Never heard of him," said a third.

Kit grinned at them. "Ignoramuses! He used to stay at Coldmellow during the war."

"Which one? The Boer war?" they teased.

"The Second World War," she said. "He was a pilot in the Battle of Britain. He was killed later on, but his poems are becoming very popular both here and in the States."

"I never read poetry," one young man said cheerfully. "Seed catalogues are the full extent of my reading material."

"Peasant," Andy mocked him.

A stocky young man frowned suddenly. He had spatulate hands, a rolling walk and patient brown eyes, and had told her he was a shepherd working on a farm two miles off.

"Polish, did you say? I wonder if he was the chap who used to stay with my gran?"

Kit felt a quiver of excitement, the thrill of the fisherman who feels the tug on the line. "Where did your gran live?"

"Coldmellow, of course," he said patiently. "She's mentioned a foreign chap staying with her during the war—he owed her rent when he left the last time, which made her mad. She hates to lose money due to her, my gran does."

"Where does she live?" Kit asked eagerly.

He looked at her impatiently. "I told you—Cold-mellow."

"But which house? What's the address?"

The young man looked at Andy with amusement. "Andy will show you."

Andy, his mouth crammed with chicken, nodded. When he had eaten the mouthful he said, "Of course I know old Gran Whitlow. I should have thought of her before. She still takes the odd visitor, and she does teas in the summer."

Kit turned and searched the supper room for Adam, but he was nowhere to be seen. Otherwise occupied, no doubt, she thought with jealous irritation. Well, he would have to wait to hear this news. Serve him right.

When they left the supper room they met Adam and Anthea arriving. Anthea flipped pink-tipped fingers at them casually.

"Is the food good?"

"Great," Andy said enthusiastically. He had an arm round Kit's waist to forestall any dispute over his possession of her as a partner.

"See you, then," Anthea dismissed, sweeping past without so much as a look at Kit.

Adam moved aside to let Kit pass, and their eyes met at close quarters. He looked impassive, his features unreadable. Her glance dropped away almost at once. She did not want him to see her feelings written in her face.

Several dances later she was beginning to feel wretchedly weary, her head aching, her back and ankles throbbing with the continual dancing she had subjected them to over the past few hours.

"Shall we sit this one out?" she asked Andy, who agreed with faint reservations.

"But don't dance with anyone else, will you?" he asked her anxiously.

They had been sitting in a quiet corner for five minutes when Adam strolled up.

Kit saw his approach with tingling nerves. He gave Andy a nod, then looked at her. "Time we had our dance," he said coolly.

She half meant to refuse, but in the end could not force her unwilling tongue to speak the words. Instead she stood up, to Andy's protesting words. "We were going to sit this one out..."

Adam ignored him, leading her on to the floor by the hand, then pulling her closely into his arms.

Her pulses began to leap wildly at his closeness. She danced in a sort of daze, conscious of his hand on her back, his fingers gripping hers.

They did not speak during the dance. Kit wondered if he could hear her heart beating. Her head only just came to his shoulder. She could have turned her hot face into his neck above his crisp white collar. Once Adam's hand moved slowly, stroking her back as if enjoying the silken feel of her gown. Once his chin lowered to brush the top curls on her head. Kit was lost to everything but his nearness, giving herself up to sheer sensual enjoyment of the moment.

When the music ended they drew slowly apart. She wondered if it was as hard for him to release her as it was for her to stand back from the hard circle of his arm. She hoped it was. Bitterly, she hoped his pain equalled her own. I could kill him, she thought. I could kill him for what he's doing to me, to both of us.

In sight of heaven, he refused to enter it. If he had been honest when he said he loved her, he ought to be suffering now, yet there was no sign of it on his bland face. He wore a smiling mask as he looked down at her.

"Thank you." The words were polite, almost indifferent. She could not penetrate the mask he wore.

"I think I've found Jan Watowski's landlady," she told him abruptly.

He looked interested at once. "Really? That's splendid. Is she here tonight?"

She shook her head. "No, but Andy knows where to find her."

"Then we'll go and see her tomorrow," he said. They walked across the floor. Staring straight ahead, Adam said quietly, "That dress makes you look very sexy. You're having a heady effect on the local young men, I see. You'll make Andy jealous."

"I'm having a wonderful time," she told him defiantly.

He looked down at her and smiled suddenly, his dark face full of tender amusement which took her breath away. "Are you, indeed? You shameless hussy!"

She laughed back at him, melting under his sunshine smile. "It isn't often I get the chance to play the peacock."

"Be careful you don't get your feathers pulled out by jealous local maidens. I've seen some very nasty looks aimed at your back."

She giggled. "So have I. They'll get over it."

The band crashed into the last dance, a Paul Jones, and Andy dragged her away to join the linked circle of girls. Passing round to the music she came face to face with Adam again. He grinned as he danced her away.

"Twice in ten minutes," he murmured in her ear. "This is getting to be a habit."

"Then you had better be careful, hadn't you?" she teased.

His arm tightened, making her gasp. Then the music switched to the Paul Jones again, and they separated. Kit danced the next two dances with strangers, making polite conversation.

The drive home was cheerful. Andy sang as he drove them, his voice husky with tiredness. Adam relaxed in the back with Kit, staring out into the darkness. She lay with closed lids, longing for sleep.

She almost fell into her bed and slept deeply until well into the morning. When she did wake up it was to hear a church bell intoning deeply somewhere on the hill above. She sat up, yawning. Looking at her clock, she groaned at the time. Eleven o'clock! She leapt out of bed and grabbed up her dressing-gown. The bathroom was luckily empty. She washed and then dashed back to get dressed.

She found Adam reading the Sunday papers over the remains of a hearty breakfast. He looked up wryly as she rushed into the room.

"You certainly slept well!"

"Did you call me?"

"I peeped round the door at nine, but you were dead to the world. I hadn't the heart to wake you."

"Where's Andy?"

"Seeing to some farm business, he said. He was looking dead tired when I saw him. He got up early to take a look at some ewes in a field the other side of the hill, then dashed off again on some other errand. Obviously never a dull moment in farming.''

Kit poured herself some lukewarm coffee, nibbled a piece of rather scorched toast. ''Are we going to see this woman today?''

''When you're ready,'' he said coolly.

She drank the coffee with a grimace, then stood up. ''I'm ready,'' she told him.

''We'll leave a note for Andy. He told me which house she lived in and I said we would pop round there.''

They walked up the hill along a narrow, high-banked lane made bright with pink campion and willowherb. A lark sang high above them on the green downland and the sheep grazed patiently on the short grass.

''This is the house,'' Adam said, pausing to study the tiny gabled building with interest. A farm-labourer's cottage, built somewhere around the end of the nineteenth century, it stood in a cottage garden filled with sweet williams, stocks, great white daisies and marigolds. The roof was thatched with dark brown reeds patchy with age. The walls were white-washed, solid and weather-worn. The front door stood open, revealing a small linoleumed passage and beyond that a kitchen. A woman sat on the whitened step, a metal colander in her aproned lap, shelling peas. As they pushed open her gate she looked up and stared at them, her black eyes beady with hard interest.

She was in her seventies, shrivelled and stooped, but wiry with a reserve of strength. Her iron-grey hair was neatly curled in an old-fashioned frizzy style. Her face bore no trace of make-up.

"Good morning," Adam said courteously. "Mrs. Whitlow?"

"That's me," she said quickly. "What did you want?"

"I'm doing research into the life of Jan Watowski," Adam began.

"You a copper?" the old woman demanded.

"No," he said politely. "I'm a television producer."

Her face went blank. She stared from him to Kit. "Oh, yes?" she asked derisively, obviously not believing him.

Adam sighed. He took from his jacket inside pocket a small stiff card and flipped it open to show her. It was his car park card, the one issued to the staff of the studios as security clearance and meant to be presented every time they went in to the building.

The old woman studied it for a long time. "Anyone could buy one of them," she said at last, but without conviction.

"You can ring the studios if you wish to have confirmation," Adam told her.

She shrugged. "All right, so you're a television producer. Who is this . . . what you call him?"

"Don't you recall the name?" Adam could not help showing his disappointment. "I think he may have stayed with you during the Second World War. He was a pilot in the Royal Air Force, a Polish pilot flying with them."

"Oh, that foreign chap," she said disgustedly. "I didn't remember his name. Swindled me, he did. Said he'd pay me next time he came down, said he didn't have enough cash left then, but he never came back.''

"He was killed," Adam said flatly.

"So they said," Mrs Whitlow muttered. "I went over there to see them when I was visiting my sister. She lived near his camp and I got me chance then. I had to kick up a fuss before they paid me what I was owed, though."

"But you were paid in the end?" Kit asked, pretending sympathy. "Can I give you a hand with these peas?"

Mrs. Whitlow gave her a hard look, then surrendered a lapful of pea shucks. "If you like," she said indifferently. She abandoned her own work and linked her hands over her thin knees. "He was a funny sort of chap. I remember him well enough. I would have got the money from her up the Chapel Lane, but she was away for weeks and I couldn't wait."

"Her up Chapel Lane?" Kit probed softly. "Who was that?"

Mrs. Whitlow gave a wry mimicry of a smile, drawing back her thin lips from her gums like a horse. "She was always with him. Englishmen weren't good enough for her, seemingly. Never married neither, afterwards. Eccentric, they says in the village. Proud piece, I call her. Stuck-up, like."

"Put on airs?" Kit suggested, shelling peas swiftly. Adam had leaned against the door post, leaving the interrogation to her for the moment.

"Ah, she did that. Of course, she was eddicated. Went to a paying school over to Salisbury. Her dad was in the church—Vicar over at Wilton. I never knew him, mind, but that's what she says. That niece of hers is another out of the same box. Minces about village on one of her nags with her nose in the air, too good to pass the time of day with anyone."

Kit stiffened. "Her niece?"

"That Miss Gable. Anthea . . . what a name! Who ever heard of a name like that . . ."

"What did he do while he was staying with you?" Adam asked her, his grey glance meeting Kit's as he spoke, a blaze of excited interest in it.

"When he wasn't mooning over fields with 'er, he went fishing morning, noon and night. It helped with the rationing, mind. He ate like a bird, I'll give him that. He didn't mind what you put in front of him, neither. Fish for every meal, he didn't care."

"What sort of man was he?" Kit asked.

Mrs. Whitlow gave her a disgusted look. "I told you—a foreigner of some sort."

"What did he talk about?"

"To me? Nothing. I hadn't got time for gossiping with the likes of him."

They talked to her for another ten minutes, but got no further with their enquiries, and at last left her, pursued to the gate with a demand that they pay her for her "valuable time wasted on rubbish like that . . ."

Adam strolled along with his hands in his pockets, a look of excitement on his handsome face. "So we've found our mystery woman," he said.

"Anthea's aunt," Kit murmured drily.

Adam shot her a look. "Yes," he said. "I wonder if she's anything like her niece? A beautiful svelte blonde, perhaps? I imagine a Polish poet might well go for that."

"Watowski had more taste," Kit said.

"Miaow!" Adam taunted.

Kit lifted her chin defiantly and didn't bother to answer. They walked along in silence for a bit, then Adam said to her, "I'm sure we're close to the truth now. Landell had nothing about this girl. The very fact that Jan kept her a secret must mean that there was something serious to the relationship."

"And she never married," Kit said, sighing.

Adam grimaced. "Sensible woman."

Kit felt a shiver run down her spine.

CHAPTER NINE

WHEN they returned to Andy's house they found him in the kitchen peeling potatoes clumsily with the radio blaring at his elbow. He looked round and smiled at them. "There you are!"

"I'll do that," Kit told him, seizing the potato peeler and starting work as she spoke.

"I'm afraid I'm no great hand with that particular job," Andy confessed. "I peel great chunks of potato along with the skin."

"So I see," she smiled, staring at the tiny, marble-like potatoes he had already prepared.

"What did you find out from Gran Whitlow?" he asked.

"Quite a bit," Adam told him. "Apparently Watowski used to see a lot of Anthea's aunt."

Andy looked astonished. "You're kidding!"

"So the old woman said! What is Anthea's aunt like?"

Andy shrugged. "I hardly know her. She lives at Rosemary Cottage, at the top of Chapel Lane, and she keeps cats, dozens of them. A funny old thing to look at. Hardly the femme fatale type. She's famous for herbs."

"Herbs?" Kit asked, looking up from her task. "How do you mean, herbs?"

"Unofficially, she doses local people with herbal remedies. She grows the things in her garden, makes them up in little packets and sells 'em."

"Sounds dangerous," Adam commented.

"To my knowledge she's never killed anybody, and our local doctor is a friend of hers, so he obviously doesn't mind her activities. She has a small private income, I think. Anthea is staying with her at the moment. She could introduce you." Andy gave Adam a quick, shrewd look. "I'm sure she would be helpful to you."

Kit glanced at Adam to see how he took this remark. He was looking blank, his hands in his pockets, and his eyes shielded by his drooping lids.

"I'll ring her now, if I may use your phone," he said to Andy.

"Sure. Go ahead."

Adam left the kitchen, and Andy watched him, then turned to Kit with a peculiar expression on his pleasant, fresh-complexioned face.

"Anthea seems very taken with him."

Kit hesitated, then said tentatively, "Yes. Do you mind?"

He laughed, looking taken aback. "Is it that obvious? No, I don't mind at all. On the contrary. For a while Anthea and I were...pretty friendly. But then...well, it sounds unchivalrous of me, but to be frank I got tired of the relationship. I felt she was a little too..." he looked embarrassed, "...well, too managing. If I'd thought she genuinely liked me for myself it would have been different. But I realised it was this house, the land, she really wanted. She wasn't sincere. I let it drop as delicately as I could, but Anthea isn't easy to get rid of.'' He flushed. "This sounds ghastly. I hate talking about it.''

"Then don't,'' Kit urged. "I understand.''

He looked at her gratefully. "You're a very nice person, Kit. I wish...'' He shrugged. "Well, you know what I wish.''

She smiled at him. "Do I?''

He moved closer and bent forward to kiss her lightly on the lips. "Of course you do. You're the most attractive girl I've ever known.''

She laughed, "More attractive than Anthea?'' then regretted the question. "Don't answer that. It was what is known as a leading question, wasn't it?''

"I will answer it,'' Andy said. "Yes, more attractive than any girl I've ever known, and that includes Anthea.''

Kit was touched. "Thank you, Andy.'' She reached up on tiptoe to kiss him, was caught and held tightly in a bear hug while he kissed her back.

When he released her she found herself staring straight into Adam's face. He was standing at the door watching them with narrowed eyes, his expression grim.

She hurriedly returned to her potato peeling. Andy gave Adam a faintly embarrassed grin.

"Get through all right?''

"Yes,'' said Adam tightly. "We've been invited to tea at Rosemary Cottage this afternoon.''

"Does that include me?" Andy asked a little doubtfully.

"Yes," said Adam almost viciously, "it includes you."

Andy gave him a faint, dubious smile. "Oh."

"Why don't you two go and sit down while I cook lunch?" Kit suggested. "I'll get on better without interruptions."

Lunch was rather late because Kit took so long to find the various items she needed, but at last she served it to the two men in the dining-room. It was a simple meal; lamb chops, new potatoes and peas followed by apple pie and ice-cream. The men ate heartily, forgiving her the delay, and insisted on washing up afterwards.

At three-thirty they set off for Rosemary Cottage together. Chapel Lane was a fair walk away, running from the church in a northerly direction round the hill, past a squat red-brick Methodist Chapel which was clearly a remnant of the great Victorian revival, its architecture ugly and functional. A sea of thistles and grass washed up to the walls. Green-painted iron railings surrounded it.

"There was a chapel here in the middle ages," Andy told them. "It belonged to a monastery which used to stand in the valley. Both of them vanished in the sixteenth century."

They paused to look down the hill, puffing breathlessly. Below them the green valley spread itself in the sun. Dusty white roads wound in a criss-cross fashion between villages, their progress outlined by green hedges and the pink and white blossoms of the may.

"It's surprising how many different shades of green there are," Kit commented. "Each tree and bush seems to be a different colour."

"Not bad, is it?" Andy agreed proudly. He pointed to some sheep. "Some of my flock. I've had a fair number of lambs this spring. I shall do quite well with them, I hope, touch wood." He leaned over to touch a fence superstitiously.

"Do you like sheep?" Kit asked him out of curiosity.

"I suppose I must do," he shrugged. "I've worked with them all my life. They're a bit stupid, but I get a kick out of stopping them from killing themselves. They seem determined to do so if they can—the trick is to anticipate their daft tricks and put a stop to them."

They walked on and came to a wrought-iron gate, painted white, set between posts from which spread a tall privet hedge. Beyond it lay a wild-looking garden, with narrow winding paths threading between beds of herbs and flowers and vegetables, all jumbled up together, some of them partly choked with weeds. Among the wilderness of the garden stood a tiny, octagonal cottage which looked rather like a doll's house or an old-fashioned Victorian post box. It was built of weathered red brick similar to that used in the chapel, and had a mossy red roof.

"Oh, it's delightful!" Kit cried eagerly.

"Eccentric, though," Andy said. "Like its owner."

They walked up the main path which was tiled with black and white squares edged with pieces of red tile. Celandine strayed across the path. There was a heavy scent of roses on the air. As they reached the rose-twined porch which framed the front door, Anthea came out to greet them.

"Tea is ready in the back garden," she informed them. "Come round . . ."

"Tea in the garden? How lovely," Kit said politely.

Anthea gave her a cool look. "Aunt Sorrel always eats in the garden if it's warm enough," she said reluctantly.

"Sorrel?" Kit exclaimed, looking at Adam with excitement.

He nodded back. "Yes, I noticed."

Anthea looked totally blank. It was clear that she did not know Jan Watowski's poem entitled *Sorrel*, a sonnet celebrating the plant which turns the heathlands of England rusty red in summer. There was no personal mention of any kind in the poem, but it was too much of a coincidence to be accidental. True, the poem could have been written before he met Anthea's aunt, Kit thought, but such a wild coincidence was unthinkable. Jan Watowski *must* have been discreetly flattering his girlfriend by the poem.

As they walked round the house Kit's pulses were thundering with anticipatory excitement. At last they were going to meet this mysterious heroine of the poet's life. All speculation would soon be at an end.

A white iron-work table stood on a daisy-starred lawn. Around it were grouped some chairs. In one of them sat a huge marmalade cat with half-closed eyes observing their approach. In another sat a small black kitten with four white paws and a splashy white bib. He leapt down and vanished as they arrived.

From a flower bed near by emerged a woman in a white shirt and a faded tweed skirt. Kit gazed at her curiously. Thin, slight, fragile, with high cheekbones and austere features, she had a swathe of long white hair brushed over the top of her head. Wild blue eyes gazed back at them out of the weather-browned face.

"My aunt Sorrel," Anthea said flatly, her voice bearing the faintest tinge of irritation.

For a moment no one moved or spoke, then Sorrel came forward, her hand outstretched. "How nice of you to come to tea," she said softly.

Kit moved to meet her, felt her own hand touched by one which was tiny, earth-stained and fleshless. She met the fierce blue eyes and felt the impact of an original spirit. Excitement blazed inside her. Yes, she thought, this was Jan Watowski's woman all right. Any poet, meeting this fey creature, must have been interested.

Then Adam shook hands, smiled probingly, said a few polite words. Moments later they were all seated around the table. The marmalade cat shot off crossly. Sorrel laughed and watched indulgently as he stalked off, tail swishing with reproof.

"Oliver is offended!"

"You like cats," Kit observed, accepting a plate and some tiny sandwiches which, she was sure, had been made by Anthea not her aunt.

Sorrel said gently, "I never turn a cat away. They're no trouble and they need love just like anybody else."

"Dirty, flea-ridden nuisances," Anthea snapped. She shuddered. "I hate them. They smell and leave hairs on my clothes."

Her aunt eyed her without replying. Kit nibbled her sandwich for a moment, waiting for Adam to open the questioning, but he began to talk about the herbs Andy had mentioned.

Sorrel answered cheerfully, told them what sort of preparations she made and how well they sold. "People are getting more and more interested in the natural use of herbs. Rosemary for the hair, verbena for the eyes, arnica for bruises...a hundred herbs, a hundred different uses for them."

"Do you grow them all here?" Kit asked, fascinated. She glanced around the garden. Like the one at the front of the cottage, it was laid out in beds, with paths between them. She began to notice small points—that the vegetable beds were largely clear of weeds, well tended, with care having been taken to keep the rows straight and tidy; that the flowers were grouped in great clumps, the bushes and shrubs pruned to keep a pleasing shape. Clearly, Sorrel had a purpose in making parts of her garden wild.

"I grow many herbs here," Sorrel told her. "Camomile, parsley, peppermint, valerian, lavender, rosemary, thyme, bay...and dozens of others grow wild in the woods and hedges around here. Colts-foot, elder, lovage, alder, thistle... I use them all in cosmetic preparations which are much appreciated."

"Thistle?" Kit echoed disbelievingly.

Sorrel smiled suddenly, her small austere face shining with amusement, becoming in an instant beautiful. "Did you think it had no use? All plants are useful in one way or another. Only ignorance condemns them to grow and wither without interest."

Anthea gave a brittle laugh. "Aunt Sorrel has some very weird ideas." She fluttered her lashes at Adam, inviting his sympathy. "Too many people encourage her. The amount of nonsense talked in this house by apparently sane people would amaze you! They come here to buy her little bags of weeds every day."

Her aunt watched her calmly. She did not seem to resent Anthea's scornful dismissal of her herbal practice.

"I think many modern drug houses have come to recognise the use of herbs as beneficial," Kit defended.

Sorrel glanced at her, as if pleased by this support. Anthea lifted one slim shoulder in a cold shrug.

"They make money out of superstition, you mean," she retorted.

"What is penicillin but a green mould growing in a natural way? At one time scientists scoffed at the old wives' tales about mould being helpful in curing certain injuries, but it turned out to be quite true, and the discovery opened up a whole new chapter in medical history. We wouldn't have modern antibiotics if someone had not found out how nature could help to cure certain illnesses." Kit could not help her voice growing fierce, her cheeks hot with irritation at Anthea's attitude. How much of her anger was due to jealousy she did not ask herself. Instinctively she aligned herself with Sorrel against her niece.

Sorrel nodded. "Perfectly true, and I could give you a hundred similar examples. Despite all modern advances, doctors still use digitalis, a preparation made from the foxglove plant, to control heart trouble; they still use cascara as a laxative, and arrowroot to soothe digestive problems."

"They know what they're doing, though," Anthea said spitefully. "They're trained professionals. You aren't, are you?"

"I've used herbs all my life," Sorrel said. "I've studied them in books and at first hand. When you had a cough last winter you didn't refuse to take my honey, lemon and horehound mixture, did you?"

"Vile stuff," Anthea shrugged.

They finished their tea and at Sorrel's suggestion moved their chairs back from the table. She herself sprawled easily on the lawn, enjoying the sunshine on her face, screwing up her eyes in defence. Kit joined her, sitting cross-legged among the daisies, and Andy cheerfully plumped himself down beside her. Adam and Anthea, however, remained in their chairs, watching them coolly.

"I think Anthea must have told you why we're here," Adam began gently.

Sorrel shielded her eyes with one tiny hand, and looked up at him without reply.

"We're making a programme about Jan Watowski."

Anthea smiled. "I didn't even know you knew him, Aunt Sorrel."

"What makes you think I did?" Sorrel enquired softly; her face masked by that brown hand.

"This is a small village," Adam told her carefully.

She sighed. "The tongue of rumour louder than the bells? Of course . . . how long people remember such things! I suppose it's because so little happens from one year to the next. They hoard memories as squirrels hoard nuts.'' She sat up. ''And what do they say of Jan and myself?''

Adam glanced at Kit, his expression divided. She sensed that he was finding this interrogation hard. Sorrel had a dignity which made their interest seem vulgar, their curiosity common prying.

Gently she said, ''Can we tell you the story from the beginning? Our side of it, I mean?''

Sorrel looked seriously at her. ''Of course, my dear. What is your side of it?''

Quietly, Kit explained how they had taken over the programme, become convinced that Landell's book did not contain all the truth about Watowski, had tracked down Watowski's old comrades, found about the visits to Coldmellow during the war and from Gran Whitlow found out about Sorrel herself.

Sorrel listened gravely, her eyes fixed on the sky. Her lips twisted wryly as Kit tactfully skimmed over what Gran Whitlow had told them.

''I can imagine the rest,'' she interrupted. ''What do you want to know? You've met Jan's friends. What can I tell you that they could not?''

Adam opened his lips, then closed them, looking helplessly at Kit. This sign of sensitivity in him touched and moved her. She said to Sorrel, ''You can tell us whatever you think we should know.''

Sorrel sighed. ''Ah, that's easy. You already know all that Jan would have wanted you to know.''

Adam moved restlessly.

Kit glanced at him, then said, ''Did he love you, Sorrel?''

There was a silence. Sorrel stared at a wild pink rambling rose which fell in fragrant clouds from a fan-shaped support, the flowers fully open, their golden hearts showering the air with pollen. A bumble bee fumbled from flower to flower, drunk with sunshine.

"We loved each other," Sorrel said at last, so faintly that they had to crane to hear her. "For that one summer we plummeted to the ocean depths of love. Then he was killed. Finis."

Anthea was staring, torn between amazement and embarrassment, her expression funny in its sheer horror of naked emotion.

"There are gaps in the published poems," Kit said. "Not very obvious gaps—Landell was clever. But it was obvious that there were poems left out. Why?"

"I never met Landell," said Sorrel. "How should I know?"

"But you do know," Kit said reluctantly, with sympathy. "I'm sure you do."

Sorrel looked at her for a very long moment, then smiled. "My dear, you're very kind. Yes, there are gaps, and there always will be. There were some poems Jan would not have wanted published."

"Personal ones?"

"Very private ones."

"Written to you?"

Sorrel laughed. "Oh, not what you're thinking! I wouldn't be ashamed of our love. Neither would Jan. But there are some things not meant for public consumption, some things too private to be broadcast to the world."

"With all respect," Adam broke in urgently, "that argument would have meant that Shakespeare's sonnets, Keats' poems, even some of Byron's work must be left to crumble to dust unread. A great writer always writes for posterity. He writes because he needs to communicate—often he finds a response long after death in the minds of sympathetic readers who never knew him. No artist should be condemned to oblivion without having the chance to find that response."

"Jan will never be condemned to oblivion," Sorrel said with quiet certainty. "The published poems will see to that."

"But if you have other poems, the world should see them," Adam pressed her.

"What makes you think I have them?" she replied.

Adam smiled. "Landell doesn't have them or he would have published them. He deliberately left out references to you because he didn't want anyone else to know about the unpublished work. I suspect he's tried to get the poems from you and failed."

She looked amused. "You're a shrewd observer of human nature. Yes, Landell tracked me down and tried to persuade me to hand over all the papers, but I refused."

Adam sighed with satisfaction. "I knew he was hiding something! He hopes to get his hands on them one day, of course, and doesn't want anyone else to share his possession of Watowski."

"Poor Landell," said Sorrel. "How angry he'll be when he sees your programme.

"Will you agree to be interviewed?" Adam asked her.

She shook her head. "No. I never watch television—I don't possess a set. I couldn't possibly appear on the programme. I'm sorry."

"I shall have to film in the village," Adam warned.

Sorrel looked disturbed. "Oh, no! Please..."

Kit shifted uncomfortably. She looked around the wild, tranquil garden. Once the cruel eye of television had pried upon this little world the curious sightseers would come to stare from a distance at Sorrel's cottage.

"I have no alternative," Adam said uncompromisingly. "I quite understand your desire for privacy, but try to see it from my point of view. Watowski is increasingly admired as a poet. Everything about him is important. The background of his poems has to be evaluated. You are a very important part of that background. I suspect the poems you have may be of vital significance to understand him."

Sorrel shook her head. "No! You don't understand..."

"Make me, then. Let me see the poems. Let me make my own decision about them." He looked penetratingly at her. "Has Landell seen them?"

She smiled. "No."

"Ah..." Adam looked triumphant. "Then only you know the hidden truth about Jan Watowski."

Sorrel clasped her hands together and stared at them. "Who ever knows the whole truth about anyone?"

"You know more than the rest of us, at any rate," Adam said.

Anthea was frowning. "You would pay very well, I suppose? I mean, television does, doesn't it? And if it's so necessary to your programme?" She gave her aunt a placatory smile. "Well, you aren't exactly rich, are you, Aunt Sorrel? You could do with a little more money. Well, anyone could."

Her aunt regarded her sadly. "Oh, Anthea, my dear—as if money had any significance!"

Anthea flushed at her tone. "You have to eat. You can't eat poetry."

"I live very well," Sorrel assured her. "I'm sorry, Mr. Rothbury, if I'm upsetting your plans, but my private life is my own concern and nobody else's. I can't appear on your programme and I will never let anyone see Jan's poems."

Adam stared at her hard. "Then why haven't you destroyed them?"

She looked taken aback.

"You haven't, have you?" Adam spoke flatly. "You still read them from time to time. That seems rather selfish, don't you think? You have access to a public treasure and you're denying others the chance to find Jan Watowski for themselves..."

"Selfish?" She looked distressed. "Oh, no, I don't think so. You don't understand."

"Give me the chance to understand, then."

She stood up, shaking her head. "I'm sorry, no. Selfish or not, I can't let anyone else see the poems. Goodbye, Mr. Rothbury. Please don't come again. I don't want to have endless arguments with you. I hope you will respect my wishes—I wouldn't want to get angry with you."

"As you did with Landell?" he guessed.

She sighed. "Yes, in the end I did. He was too persistent. I assure you, I shan't change my mind. Landell tried hard, but even he saw that I meant what I said in the end. Tenacity is my chief virtue, I think."

Adam stood up, too, his stance remorseless. "I can't promise to stay away," he said. "My own attitude is just as determined as yours, Miss Gable."

"I will not see you," she said gently. "So please do as I ask. Leave me alone, or I may have to call the police. I can refuse to admit you to my property, you know. You have no right to enter here."

Adam stared at her, his face like granite. "I hope you won't take such an attitude."

"Don't force me to do so, then," she replied. "Anthea, see them to the gate and lock it behind them." She turned and vanished into the wilderness of the garden, disappearing into a tangle of apple trees at the far end.

Anthea gave Adam a sympathetic grimace. "She's as stubborn as a mule. I'll try to talk her round. Don't worry."

"I'll be very grateful if you could," Adam said eagerly. "Quite frankly, I think it would be public-spirited of you to do so. Those poems don't belong to one person. They belong to the world. They may well be Watowski's greatest work—they must be the last work he ever did, and he was still so young when he died. Just think! If someone had suppressed the work Keats did in his last three months on earth we would lose some of his most beautiful work."

Anthea nodded agreement. "I'll do whatever I can." She looked at the cottage curiously. "I wonder where she keeps them. I've never seen her reading them. She's very secretive."

She and Adam walked ahead, talking quietly. Kit and Andy came together in the rear. Kit looked at Adam's back with a sense of bitter regret. She knew that what he said was true, yet she could not help feeling a deep sympathy with Sorrel Gable. In her position, Kit thought, I would very likely do the same thing. Love is private. It should not be dragged out into public view.

CHAPTER TEN

ADAM took Anthea out that evening, leaving Kit and Andy to amuse themselves. Andy suggested that they drive into the nearest town to see a film, but Kit was quite happy to spend a quiet evening at the house.

"We could play cards," she suggested.

"Wouldn't you find that dull?" Andy looked surprised.

"We spent such a hectic day yesterday," she pointed out. "The drive down here, then the dance...I'm a little tired."

"Well, if you're sure," he agreed. "What shall we play?"

They played gin rummy for matches, the prize for the final winner being a box of chocolates Andy produced from somewhere. Kit's mind was not on the game. Andy won, and ceremonially opened the chocolates. They sat on the carpet listening to a recent recording of Lehár's operetta *The Merry Widow*, eating chocolates in a growing twilight. It grew quite chilly, and Andy switched on an electric fire. It had mock logs arranged in front of it, and their orange glow gave the room a romantic look. It suited the music.

When Adam returned alone he found them still there, leaning against each other sleepily in front of the fire, the dark room filled with the flickering light, the record player still giving out the sweet, romantic music.

Kit glanced up to see him framed in the door, a menacing, rigid stillness in his attitude, watching them.

Then with a flick of his hand he brutally put on the light. They were shaken out of their sleepy content. Blinking, they shook themselves and stood up.

"Oh, hello," Andy yawned. "My God, look at the time! I had no idea it was so late. I must go to bed. I've got to be up early."

"I'll make some cocoa," Kit offered.

Andy shook his head. "Not for me, thanks, but do make some for yourself. Goodnight . . ."

He nodded to Adam and left them. Kit walked through the dark, cold passage to the kitchen and put on some milk in a saucepan. Adam followed her. He was wearing a white fisherman's sweater and casual cords. He looked big and masculine, leaning against the wall. She was deeply aware of him there, but her jealous resentment was such that she ignored him. He had been with Anthea all evening. She hoped he had enjoyed himself. No doubt Anthea had been eager to please. She found Adam's glamour appealing.

The milk seethed. Kit deftly mixed the cocoa and handed Adam a large mug of it. She took her own drink back to the sitting-room and crouched in front of the fire, feeling chilled to the bone. Emotion was draining, she thought, staring at the artificial flames.

Adam stalked towards her and stood, his eyes fixed on her slight figure, towering above her.

"You two made a very romantic picture in the fire-light," he said. "A pity the romance was as phony as the log fire."

"I like Andy," she said quietly.

"Like!" Adam snorted. "A milk-and-water word for a milk-and-water emotion."

"Leave me alone, Adam," she told him in sudden fury.

"Let you wreck your life, you mean?" he demanded. "You would be bored to death in a few weeks if you married someone like Andy."

"That's my business."

"No," he denied savagely, "it's mine."

"You have no right to make it yours," she said miserably. "You're too frightened to risk real emotional involvement yourself. You certainly have no right to interfere with my own choice of a life partner."

He watched her drain the last of her cocoa and set the mug down. She stood up to go to bed. Adam caught her by the shoulders in a savage movement, holding her too tightly for escape. His dark face glared down at her, the steely eyes narrowed.

"I won't let you do such a stupid thing as tie yourself to that boy..."

"You won't let me?" she laughed bitterly. "You can't stop me!"

"Can't I?" His fingers bit into her shoulders. "We'll see about that!"

The sound of footsteps broke into their absorbed concentration of each other. Adam released her and turned to glare at the door. To their astonishment it was not Andy who pushed it open, but Anthea, wrapped in a suede jacket, her air conspiratorial. She was carrying a large cardboard box.

"I've got them!" she announced triumphantly, holding out the box to Adam.

He moved eagerly to take it, his face ablaze with excitement. "My God, how did you persuade her to change her mind? This is marvellous!" He put the box on the table, lifted the lid reverently.

Kit was frowning, her intuition working feverishly. "Adam," she said quickly, "don't look at them."

He turned to stare at her in stunned disbelief. "What the hell do you mean? Don't be stupid, Kit. Why shouldn't I?"

Kit looked at Anthea challengingly. "I don't believe Sorrel Gable gave Anthea these. Did she, Anthea?"

Adam looked at Anthea, eyes narrowed. "Nonsense! Anthea wouldn't take them without permission." Then, seeing the other girl's coldly stubborn expression, he added less certainly, "You didn't just take them without permission, did you?"

"Why not?" Anthea retorted. "You said they didn't belong to her but to the world! She had no more right to keep them than I have. They should be published. Anyway, I read some of them, and they're a mess—crossed out and written over, some of them not even finished. There are letters there, too. Some of them are love letters, but a lot of them are feeble letters about him being scared stiff in the air. He was a terrible coward, after all. He hated flying and dreaded going up every night." Anthea looked scornfully at

Adam. "All your theories about him being such a great hero are washed out, believe me. He was lily-livered!"

Adam stared at her, his expression unreadable, then he looked down at the cardboard box.

"In my opinion it's time everyone knew the truth about him, anyway," Anthea said. "Remember, you promised to help me get work in television training horses for films. That was what we agreed. I kept my part of the bargain, I got you the papers. You've got to keep yours."

"Adam!" Kit was shocked and disgusted. "You didn't promise to do that in exchange for the papers, did you? My God, how low can you sink? It makes me sick to think of it, I refuse to be a party to this. I'm going round to tell Miss Gable that you've stolen her papers. The police will make you give them back. You can't be allowed to do this."

"You mind your own business," Anthea snapped, turning on her viciously. "You're pathetic, do you know that? You're just jealous because Adam finds me attractive. It's so obvious it's funny! My God, how Adam must pity you! If you had any damned pride you'd clear out and leave us to sort this out."

Kit walked to the door stiffly, feeling sick in her stomach. There was just enough truth in what Anthea said to make the words sting.

"Adam!" Anthea's exclamation made her turn and stare. She saw Adam ramming the lid back on the cardboard box, watched as he felt in his pocket, found a piece of string and tied the box firmly. "What are you doing?" Anthea demanded. "Don't take any notice of her! She's a sentimental fool."

"I'll drive you and the box back to the cottage," Adam told her calmly.

"I'm not going back." Anthea flung at him. "My cases are in my own car outside. I won't be welcome at Rosemary Cottage again, and that doesn't bother me a bit, because my aunt is a silly, pathetic woman, with her herbs and her cats and her cowardly boyfriend..."

Adam stared at her gravely. The cold, beautiful face was transformed with malice and hatred. Anthea looked suddenly ugly.

She snatched at the box. "And I'll take that!" she spat furiously. "It's worth money. Landell will pay if you won't..."

Adam caught her arm in an iron grip, unpeeled her fingers from the box and then handed the box to Kit. "Take it out to the car," he said. "I want to speak to Anthea alone."

She obeyed silently. The darkness was chilly and menacing out here in the countryside, far from the street lights of a town, with the great starry sky wheeling overhead, stretching out to fathomless space. Kit sat in the car, waiting for Adam. Out in the dark a fox cried protestingly, a sad and lonely sound. There were rustlings in the grass and hedges, the whispering of trees and the sudden flap of an owl's wing as it sailed from the roof. Andy had warned her that owls nested in one of the barns. He had even shown her a white owl face up among the beams, fleeing the light and their intrusive presence. "They keep the mice down," Andy had said. "The mice make havoc with my stores if they're left to get on with it. I'm happy to have owls around."

She held the cardboard box tenderly. It contained the private, secret life of a great poet. The thought of displaying Jan Watowski's fear and love to the curious, avid eyes of the world made her shiver in protest as much as had that fox out in the darkness. What had Sorrel said? That there were some things not meant for others to see? Even poets had a right to some privacy. Words echoed in her brain. "The grave's a fine and private place..."

Adam climbed in beside her and slammed the door. Without a word he started the engine. With a roar, another car started at the same time and shot past them, blaring an angry hooter. Anthea disappeared into the darkness like a meteor, her tail lights orange.

Kit sighed deeply. Adam edged slowly down the drive and out into the road beyond.

They were at Rosemary Cottage a few minutes later. There were lights shining in the lower windows. The door opened before they knocked. Sorrel stood framed in the yellow light.

Silently Adam handed her the box. She stared at him searchingly, her fingers finding the string and touching it.

"I didn't read a word," Adam said soberly. "I brought them back at once."

She sighed, the sound wrenched from her. "I knew she'd taken them when I heard her drive away so late at night. I've been sitting here in despair..." Her face was white beneath the tan, her eyes haunted.

"I'm afraid she read some of them," Adam said gently.

"Ah!" Sorrel's sigh was deep. "I wondered if she had. Well, come in . . ."

"No, not now," Adam said. "I'm sorry you've been hurt like this. It's my fault. I put the idea into her head. I didn't intend that she should steal them, of course, but I did want her to press you to agree to let me see them, so I'm directly responsible for this. I'm afraid she may go to Landell with what she knows. She may even have extracted one or two—I wouldn't put it past her. She's unscrupulous."

"Yes," said Sorrel, "I know. Her parents spoiled her. Beauty is often a snare. Jan once said that beauty is a pit into which we fall helplessly. At the end he came to value a different sort of beauty—the stark skeleton beneath the skin, he called it. As a boy he had loved summer and flowers, the richness of physical beauty. Before he died he turned aside from that to seek eternity."

Adam watched her austere, impassioned face regretfully. "What a pity you'll never make that programme," he said. "You're probably the best monument he left behind him."

A strange, startled expression came into her face. "That's a very kind thing to say," she said. "Thank you."

"Goodnight," Adam said gently. "And goodbye."

She held out her hand. "Goodbye."

He shook his hand, then stalked away. Kit hesitated, then flung her arms around Sorrel and kissed her. "Goodbye," she whispered. "And...I'm glad it's like this...I'm glad."

Sorrel hugged her back. "Must it be goodbye between us?" She held Kit warmly, looking into her face. "You're very sensitive, my dear. I took to you at once. You love that man, don't you? Don't bother to answer. It is written all over you. Don't let him escape you. He needs you. Life is too short for pride or fear. Jan and I faced both and defeated them utterly."

"He...conquered his fear in the end?" Kit asked her tentatively.

She nodded, her face alight. "Before he died he knew death for what it is...a consummation, not a terror."

"Then why won't you let the world learn from his experience?" Kit asked very gently. "If he'd been defeated it would have been understandable, but surely his victory should be clearly celebrated?"

Sorrel gazed at her in still silence for a long moment, then with a strange, proud gesture of acquiescence, she put the box into her hands. "You're right. Take them. Use them as you think wisest, and then bring them back to me yourself. I give them into your keeping, my dear. I trust you."

Kit felt tears prick at her eyes. "Are you sure? Quite sure?"

"My dear, if Anthea read some of them she'll certainly try to make capital of her knowledge. It's better that the world should know the whole truth than hear a mangled half truth from Landell. And you've convinced me that I was wrong to hide Jan's struggle with fear all these years. He was a man, not a god. His humanity is his strength. I've been mistaken, but I will put it right now."

Kit held the box close to her breast. "I'll look after them, I swear it, and we'll handle the story as sensitively as we know how."

She kissed Sorrel again, then followed Adam back to the car. He was sitting in the driver's seat, his head in his hands. Kit climbed in beside him.

"I've been a damned fool," he said, his voice muffled.

"So you have," Kit said cheerfully.

He sat up and turned to look at her, then stiffened as he saw what she held.

"What the..."

"She changed her mind," Kit said.

"But why...how? What on earth did you say to make her do it?"

"I convinced her, I suppose, that Jan still had something to tell us all. As you said to her, writers need to communicate. These poems and letters are a cry for understanding. He meant them to be read, not just by her but by everyone. He was an ordinary man as well as a poet, and it's as an ordinary man that he can help others to come to terms with their own fear and conquer it as he did."

Adam put out a hand and touched the box. "It will take weeks to sort through all that. May I help you?" He sounded oddly humble.

"We'll do it together," she said.

He started the car. "Thank you," he muttered, without looking at her.

They drove back through the darkness, and to Kit the chill had left the air, the menace had left the empty sky. She felt as if the night was full of singing.

They carefully locked the box away in the wardrobe of her bedroom for safety, then went back downstairs, feeling suddenly weary, yet so excited that neither could bear to sleep yet.

Kit made some more cocoa, switched on the electric fire again and sat down in front of it, toasting her fingers at its glow. Weeks of intense work lay before them. Her mind tingled at the thought of it. She had grown to feel personally involved with Jan Watowski. She could not wait to read those other poems.

"It will be like being the first man on the moon," she said suddenly to Adam. "Apart from Sorrel nobody else has ever seen these things. We'll be the first..."

"Frightening, isn't it?" Adam said sombrely.

"But thrilling!"

He stared at the firelit angles of her profile. Suddenly he said, "I love you like hell, Kit."

The deep ache of his voice made her turn instinctively. Adam made a sound of anguish and pulled her towards him, his mouth searching and finding hers. Her lips opened hungrily beneath the pressure of his, her hands crept upwards, clinging to him. Passion flared between them instantaneously, growing like a forest fire, until they were both overwhelmed with it. His hands moved hotly over her body, caressing her, arousing her to a pitch beyond which she had never been before. She gasped again and again, kissing him fiercely, feeling his control snap and his desire burst ragingly out of the bounds he had set upon it.

He pulled her on to his lap, his mouth moving down to her throat and his hands slid under her sweater, his fingers trembling as they felt the smoothness of her breasts.

"Darling, if you knew how much I want you," he muttered hoarsely.

"Love me..." she moaned, abandoning thought. "Adam...love me..."

Their mouths met again with the hard impact of a collision, she let her fingers wander over his shoulders, slid them down until they could creep like mice under his thick sweater and touch the hard walls of his naked chest.

"Go on," she whispered, as he paused to look down at her. "Don't stop..."

Adam groaned. "God help me, darling, I must or I'll lose my head altogether. You're too desirable, and I want you too much. You'll regret this in the morning, and I don't want you to regret anything."

Dry-mouthed, she clung to him, her mouth turned invitingly up to him. "I shan't regret a thing," she insisted. "I don't care about anything but you. I love you, Adam. I don't care whether we get married or not. I love you."

"You're over-excited," he said gently. "I can't take advantage of that." He lifted her off his lap and stood up. "Kit, we must go to bed. You're half asleep, too tired to know what you're doing."

She flung herself back into his arms, clutching him. "Don't you want me? Is that it?"

"Want you?" He caught her fast and buried his face hungrily in her neck. Against her skin he whispered, "I would walk barefoot through fire to be able to make love to you tonight...but I've learnt something from Jan Watowski. I want my love to be for ever." He held her away from him and looked at her soberly. "Dearest, I'm still a coward. I'm afraid of marriage. I'm terrified of committing myself to a life-long relationship. But I know something now that I didn't know before...we have to take risks sometimes. We have to gamble for our lives. If we're cowards we lose everything anyway. I've been a coward until tonight. I've been afraid of getting my fingers burnt, when all the time I was in far worse danger of losing you, the only woman I've ever loved." He lifted her hands and kissed the palms adoringly. "I'm still afraid—I won't pretend I'm not. But now I have the courage to face my fear and take the risk all the same. That's the courage Jan Watowski has given me. So will you take the risk with me? Marry me as soon as possible?"

She closed her eyes in relief and happiness. "Adam...oh, yes, yes..."

He held her face between his two hands and kissed her on the eyes, then on the mouth, lingeringly. "And no more flirting," he said teasingly. "You almost drove me wild with rage, do you know that? I was jealous enough to feel sheer hatred for that inoffensive young man."

"Poor Andy," she said.

"Poor indeed," Adam said, contentedly. "He doesn't get you, after all."

"Andy and I were friends," she said. "Nothing more. He knew how I felt about you."

Adam looked pleased with himself. "I'm relieved to hear it. So why the kissing? I caught him at it a couple of times. I wanted to smash him in the face, I may say."

Kit laughed. "You said yourself that platonic friendship doesn't exist."

He groaned. "I said too damned much, didn't I?" He eyed her broodingly. "You didn't find him attractive, did you?"

"Very attractive," she said, enjoying the feel of power he gave her.

"You tormenting witch," said Adam, squeezing her ferociously. "Don't ever let me see him kiss you again or I won't be responsible for my actions."

"What about you?" she retorted. "Flirting with Anthea?"

His face darkened. "That . . . that creature! I could have killed her for what she did tonight. What a vile thing to do. Her own aunt! It was sickening. When she asked me if I could help her get a job in television working with horses I said I might hear of something suitable and would let her know . . . I was astounded when she took this as some sort of bribe." He looked down at her seriously. "You do believe I had no intention of making such a bargain, don't you?"

"Of course I do," she nodded. "Forget about her. She isn't worth remembering." She slid her hand up his chest. "Kiss me again, Adam, kiss me hard . . ."

He kissed her until her head spun and she clung to him giddily, then drew back, breathing hard, his face flushed darkly. "This must stop," he said huskily. "We must get married soon, Kit, or I'll take possession of you without benefit of clergy, and I want our life to begin as perfectly as possible. Total, unshadowed bliss is what you shall have if I can make it so..."

"I've got that now," she said contentedly. "Don't you feel it too?" she asked, smiling up at him with sunny eyes.

"There speaks sweet innocence," he said mockingly. "If you really knew what I was feeling, my darling, you'd be shocked to the core."

She shook her head. "I'm not that innocent," she protested. "I do know...and I feel the same. It won't be long. I don't want a grand wedding. We can get married as soon as we've told J.K. the news. He'll be surprised."

"Not him," Adam grinned. "He's too clever to be unaware of how things are between us. And as for grand weddings...I want to see you in white lace and orange blossom on our wedding day. I want an organ and a choir and all the traditional things. No hole and corner job for us. I want the world to see that you belong to me for ever and ever, amen."

She eyed him incredulously. "This is a sudden conversion! Are you sure?"

"As sure as I am that if you don't get some sleep soon I shall have to carry you upstairs," he said, lifting her to her feet again. "Come on...tomorrow is the first day of a new world."

She felt her heart lift joyously. "The first day of our life," she whispered as they went upstairs hand in hand.

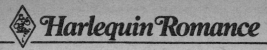
✦ Harlequin Romance

Coming Next Month

2809 THE TULLAGINDI RODEO Kerry Allyne
What's a rich girl to do when the Australian bush guide she
falls in love with thinks she's a spoiled brat? Why, get what
she wants, of course, and let him see the woman she
really is.

2810 RIDE A WILD HORSE Jane Donnelly
Twenty-two years old and longing for adventure. But it's
foolhardy for a young woman to fall for the wildly
confident organizer of an archaeological dig near her
Cotswold village if he'll only be around for the summer.

2811 SWEET PRETENDER Virginia Hart
Reluctantly, a young vacationer goes along with her sister's
masquerading as the daughter of a former Connecticut
resident. But she regrets her complicity when the pretense
stands in the way of her love.

2812 NEVER TOUCH A TIGER Sue Peters
A trapeze artist's life swings upside down when she comes
up against an arrogant English lord who threatens her
uncle's circus—not to mention her heart.

2813 UNLIKELY LOVERS Emily Spenser
A graduating botany student knows her idol has had his fill
of adoring young students. Still, she sets out to win his
respect in the hope that one day he'll make room in his
life for love.

2814 PERFUMES OF ARABIA Sara Wood
Normally, this English schoolteacher hates men like Tarik—
masterful, dynamic and ruthless. But his desert country
mesmerizes her with its timeless magic—as does the man.

Available in January wherever paperback books are sold, or
through Harlequin Reader Service.

In the U.S.
P.O. Box 1397
Buffalo, N.Y.
14240-1397

In Canada
P.O. Box 603
Fort Erie, Ontario
L2A 9Z9

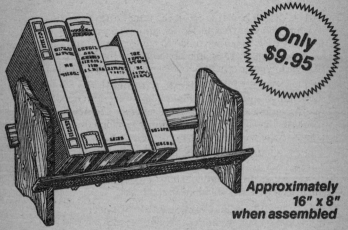

Six exciting series for you every month... from Harlequin

Harlequin Romance·
The series that started it all

Tender, captivating and heartwarming...
love stories that sweep you off to faraway places
and delight you with the magic of love.

◆

Harlequin Presents·
Powerful contemporary love stories...as individual as the women who read them

The No. 1 romance series...
exciting love stories for you, the woman of today...
a rare blend of passion and dramatic realism.

◆

Harlequin Superromance®
It's more than romance...
it's Harlequin Superromance

A sophisticated, contemporary romance-fiction
series, providing you with a longer,
more involving read...a richer mix of complex plots,
realism and adventure.

Harlequin
American Romance™
Harlequin celebrates the American woman...

...by offering you romance stories written about American women, by American women for American women. This series offers you contemporary romances uniquely North American in flavor and appeal.

◆

Harlequin Temptation
Passionate stories for today's woman

An exciting series of sensual, mature stories of love...dilemmas, choices, resolutions... all contemporary issues dealt with in a true-to-life fashion by some of your favorite authors.

◆

Harlequin Intrigue
Because romance can be quite an adventure

Harlequin Intrigue, an innovative series that blends the romance you expect... with the unexpected. Each story has an added element of intrigue that provides a new twist to the Harlequin tradition of romance excellence.

Harlequin Books

PROD-A-2

Janet Dailey Americana

Don't miss a single title from this great collection. The first eight titles have already been published. Complete and mail this coupon today to order books you may have missed.

Harlequin Reader Service

In U.S.A.
901 Fuhrmann Blvd.
P.O. Box 1397
Buffalo, N.Y. 14140

In Canada
P.O. Box 2800
Postal Station A
5170 Yonge Street
Willowdale, Ont. M2N 6J3

Please send me the following titles from the Janet Dailey Americana Collection. I am enclosing a check or money order for $2.75 for each book ordered, plus 75¢ for postage and handling.

_____	ALABAMA	Dangerous Masquerade
_____	ALASKA	Northern Magic
_____	ARIZONA	Sonora Sundown
_____	ARKANSAS	Valley of the Vapours
_____	CALIFORNIA	Fire and Ice
_____	COLORADO	After the Storm
_____	CONNECTICUT	Difficult Decision
_____	DELAWARE	The Matchmakers

Number of titles checked @ $2.75 each = $_____

N.Y. RESIDENTS ADD
   APPROPRIATE SALES TAX $_____

Postage and Handling $___.75___

                   TOTAL $_____

I enclose _____

(Please send check or money order. We cannot be responsible for cash sent through the mail.)

PLEASE PRINT

NAME _____

ADDRESS _____

CITY _____

STATE/PROV. _____

BLJD-A-1